# Every Time
# I Close My Eyes

T.R. Baker

ISBN-10: 0985764708
ISBN-13:978-0-9857647-0-8

# Memoriam

Willie Baker, Sr.
April 27, 1922 - August, 2003

Hattie Beatrice Baker
November 11, 1924 - November 2004

Hattie Mae Brown
February 11, 1919 - February, 2007

# ACKNOWLEDGMENTS

First of all, I want to say thank you to everyone that read *Every Time I Close My Eyes* the first time it was published in 2003, as well as the independent book stores that carried it. I really didn't know anything about writing, but as a result of getting published, and because of your encouragement and positive feedback, I took the time to learn everything I could to improve my writing skills. That would include joining BWWP (Black Writers With Purpose) and AWC (Atlanta Writers Club). I would encourage all novice (and experienced) writers to join organizations where they can find moral support and receive the benefit of the expertise of published authors (fiction and non-fiction), agents, copyright attorneys, book store owners, editors, and publishing companies.

I especially want to thank Taurus L. Stinnett. He is one of the nicest people I've ever met. I appreciate that you saw me as more than just a crazy lady stopping you in a hallway asking to take your photograph. Tomira Rosser, my sister/friend. As I type this, you're still waiting for me to send you information for my website. I love you and thank you for working well under pressure. Leo Sullivan, if I don't thank you I will never hear the end of it. You encourage me to write, but at the same time drive me crazy! I also thank: Michelle Beck for marking up the book I gave her and providing great advice; Chaz Cross for reading my unfinished stories and asking for more; Pamela Williams for asking me as often as possible if I'm writing; Alex Malone for telling me if my male characters really act and sound like men; Willa Dickerson for reading the story and telling me I should write; Leatha Griffin for letting me read to her over the phone, and then providing the appropriate reactions as I read; and the 556 Book Chicks (Monika, Tiffany, & Benita) for being my first reviewers. There are, for sure, more folks to thank. I'll get you on the next go around.

# Prologue

July 31, 2012. I never thought I'd find myself here, a divorcee. An attorney friend of mine once told me: "No matter how amicable a divorce is it's still very sad." She was right. I'm glad that part of my life is behind me. Still, I'm a little sad it had to end this way. There was a time when I thought getting a divorce was the worst possible thing that could happen to me, aside from death of course, but apparently it's not. I'm still breathing. I thought I'd be devastated by it, but I'm not, just unexpectedly sad. Now that it's over, it's just over.

Before today, I was able to use 'still married' as a way to avoid starting a new relationship, but now that I'm divorced I have to face my own ugly truth, which is I'm afraid of being hurt again. I have to get over it, though, because…well, I have to. I don't want to grow old alone. I don't want to rush into anything either.

So, the thing to do tonight is to forget about all of that and treat myself to a couple of drinks and a nice dinner. I hadn't done that in a long time. Heaven knows my husband never took me anywhere. But, you know what? I'm not going to go there either. My divorce was final today. Good for me.

# Chapter 1

I haven't seen my waiter in a while. Wait a minute. Who is that guy over there? He looks kind of important—tall, nice mustache, neatly trimmed haircut, dressed very nicely. He has a really nice smile too. I bet he smells good. Broad shoulders, tapered waistline—maybe he's a professional athlete? He certainly looks like someone I've seen before.

By the time I realized he was looking back at me, it was too late. I was unable to break my gaze. Good for me, though. I'm having one of my really cute days. Sometimes 5'9", pecan shell brown, slim sisters deserve to get checked out, too. I'm just going to have to play it off.

Okay, good, here comes the waiter with my salad. It's about time. He didn't seem to have a problem coming back and forth to my table to ask me if he needed to refill my wine glass. I'll just thank him and hope I don't have to wait too long for my entre. I'm going to mind my business, eat, and stop looking over at the other table. I don't want the tall, handsome guy to catch me looking at him again. You can't look at a man without him thinking you want him. I think I see my waiter, but if the food he's carrying isn't mine I'm going to have to leave and stop at Burger King on my home.

I knew I should have stopped looking over at the other table.

"Hi, I might be mistaken, but I think we had a moment...or were you flirting with me?" The stranger laughed as if he had just shared a joke with me.

I looked up at him, with his fine self. "You did cross my line of vision, so I apologize if it came across as anything other than that." I pretended to act  calm, but I wasn't.

He offered me an absolutely beautiful smile as he extended his hand. "I guess I should introduce myself. My name is Julian and I'm glad I crossed your line of vision." Again, he chuckled to himself as he spoke. "I apologize. I didn't mean to disturb you, but I really did think we had a moment."

I slowly extended my hand. "Hi, I'm Shelby. I didn't mean to disturb you either. You don't have to apologize, but you shouldn't have had to leave your dinner party to come over here."

He turned and looked back at his table. "Is it okay if I join you for dinner?"

"Are you serious?"

"Absolutely, is it okay?"

I shrugged my shoulders. "Sure…"

"Excuse me for a minute." Surprisingly, he walked over to his table, grabbed his food, and came back.

I couldn't believe it. His dinner party was as surprised as I was, but they seemed to be okay with it because they laughed and continued to enjoy their meals.

"So, Shelby, I hope this is okay. Your man could walk in at any moment and misunderstand what's going on?"

I smiled. "You don't have anything to worry about."

He wanted to know why I was there alone. I wanted to know why he was there with so many people. We did, what felt like, the normal chitchat between strangers and before we knew it we had talked for three hours. His entourage was ready to go and I really had to leave, too.

Julian asked for my phone number, so I gave him my business card and we bid our farewells. "I've never done this before, but I enjoyed dinner and the company wasn't bad either."

"What, have dinner with a stranger?"

"Well, yeah."

Then he asked me the question. "We can fix that. When can I see you again?"

I didn't want to start anything that I couldn't finish, so there was no point in seeing him again—no matter how fine he was. What did I look like starting a new relationship on the very day that I officially became single? But then again, why not today?

"I'll tell you what. I don't work too far from here, so let's say one day next week?" I shrugged my shoulders and grabbed my purse.

He smiled. "Why can't we just set a date and a time to meet? You trying to tease me or something?"

As I stood up and prepared to leave, I ignored his questions. "You know what? Wednesday or Friday will work because those are my least busiest days at work."

"Then Wednesday it is, Miss Shelby." He smiled at me mischievously, like he knew something I didn't know.

So that was that. We shook hands, he left with his friends, and I left with my pleasant memories of the evening.


The next week couldn't come fast enough. When I arrived at the restaurant Wednesday evening, guess who was already there? Julian was sitting at a nice secluded booth with a single pink rose laying on the table in front of him. That boy looked just as good as he did the first time I saw him. He smiled and stood up as I approached. He handed the rose to me as we exchanged our hellos, and then we both sat down. I ordered a glass of wine. I tried to contain how excited I was to see him again. The truth was, I had been looking forward to this moment all day.

"Well, good evening, Julian Brishard. Thank you for the rose."

"It's going to be a good evening now. I was afraid you were going to make me wait until Friday or something."

I smiled. The idea of making him wait never crossed my mind.

Our dinner was served quickly. The food was great, and the conversation was fantastic. Julian's company was even better the second time around. We spent most of the evening talking about his singing career. I knew he looked familiar. The week before I just couldn't put my finger on it. He's Jules Brishard, the neo soul singer. During dinner I learned his career was just becoming mainstream and he was working on getting his first concert schedule lined up. From what he told me, he had been singing underground for about eight years before things began to change for him. All of his hard work and discipline was finally starting to pay off. I thought it was pretty interesting that he was an entertainer type. He seemed too laid back and down to earth. Prior to meeting him, I assumed all entertainers were arrogant and high strung. Shows how much I know.

Eventually my divorce found its way into our discussion.

"So, how is it that some man divorced someone as beautiful and intelligent as you? You must be real crazy, or is there something going on with you that I just haven't seen yet?"

We both laughed.

I took a sip of wine. "You know, really, I don't know what happened. The best I can tell you is sometimes two people get married and find out that even though they both might be good people, they're just not good together. For a long time I was really unhappy and, honestly, that's an understatement. So, I guess, towards the end he was unhappy too. You know what? You don't want to hear about all of that."

I didn't want to get into any of the details of my marriage because, honestly, there are always two sides to every story.

The way Julian looked at me made me blush, so I looked away.

"I don't' mind. I'm curious. Did y'all try to make it work? What about counseling?"

I nodded. "Of course we tried counseling. Let's see, the first counselor was an older black guy." I laughed out loud. "One day, during one of my individual sessions with him, he sat on the edge of his chair and looked at me with this real stern look on his face. He told me if I was his daughter he would make me get a divorce, but because he wasn't he couldn't tell me to do that. Then he sat back in his chair and we continued with our session like he had never said a word. And, of course, there was the older black woman with the fireplace in her office. She was really nice, just like somebody's mama, but I think my ex didn't like her because she always gave us homework assignments to do. He eventually refused to go back. Oh, and there was another counselor. She was a middle-aged white woman. We didn't last long with her either."

"Why so many different ones?"

"Well, I always let him decide who we'd go see: black, white, short, tall, male, female, young, old, you know. I didn't want him to be able to use that as an excuse to end the counseling. But it always ended up being something. We ended our counseling with the first guy because he said the guy was on my side; the excuse for the second counselor was the assignments; and the excuse for the last one was…you know what? I can't even remember."

"Well, at least there wasn't another woman or anything like that."

I ate the last fork full of my meal. "There was." I spoke without looking up at him. "Let's talk about something else, okay?"

Julian smiled. "Okay, yeah, cool. Well, you know, I'm glad—I mean, I'm not glad your marriage ended, but if it hadn't we wouldn't be sitting here together. So, good for me, I think. What kind of man do you like anyway?"

It had been a long time since I thought about it. I tilted my head to one side and looked at him. "Humph, I know what I don't like. How about that?"

"I can work with that."

Before I could speak our waiter arrived with a dessert menu. Julian looked up at him. "Give us a minute, please."

"Okay, go ahead. What kind of man don't you like?"

"I don't like liars or cheaters. I guess that goes without saying. I…don't like men who are dreamers. I mean, like, dreamers who never accomplish anything. I'm all about living your dreams, but you have to put some effort behind it. Selfish men are out. I don't like fast-talkers either."

Julian laughed. "What about low talking brothers? You know, brothers who whisper when they're trying to talk to you." Then he started talking fast, barely above a whisper. "Baby, like, what's your name? I'm a Gemini."

I cracked up. "Them either."

Our waiter came back. We both stopped and looked at each other before looking up at him.

"I think I want a slice of the chocolate cake with chocolate icing. Is it a huge slice, though?"

The waiter nodded. "Yes, ma'am, it's pretty big."

"Shelby, that's what I was going to order, too. Let's share a slice."

I shrugged my shoulders. "Okay, that's fine."

Julian looked at the waiter's name tag. "Greg? Okay, Greg, would you bring us one slice of cake and a couple of forks? Thanks."

I liked everything about Julian so far. I even liked the way he took charge.

# *Chapter 2*

We continued to meet at the restaurant once a week for two months. The weeks that we didn't see each other we made sure we talked. We called each other every day, anyway, to keep up with what was going on with each other. One day, as I was sitting at a table in 'our' restaurant, waiting for Julian to arrive, a young lady, possibly in her early twenties, walked over to the table.

"Are you waiting on Jules Brishard?"

My first thought was: *Is this a groupie or is she going to threaten me and tell me she's Julian's baby's mama?*"

I chose to play ignorant. "Excuse me? Is there a problem?"

"There's no real problem, but I know someone who wouldn't appreciate you having dinner with him. So maybe you should consider leaving or something."

Baffled, I stared at her. "I see."

Then she just walked away. It was weird. The more I thought about it the more I thought she was probably just a groupie. She didn't look like the kind of woman Julian would date. She looked too young to travel in his circle. I didn't know that for sure, though. Being approached by a stranger about Julian didn't bother me, that much, but I thought Julian should know about it.

It wasn't long before he arrived.

"I apologize for being late. I got held up in a meeting at the studio."

He walked over to me and kissed me on the cheek. This was a new stage in our relationship because he had never even motioned to kiss me before today. It actually seemed like the natural thing for him to do at that moment.

From behind his back he handed me an oblong gift box. "Happy anniversary."

It had been exactly two months since we met. Even though I had gotten him a card, I didn't think a two month anniversary was the sort of thing a man kept up with.

I handed him his card. "Happy anniversary to you too."

I opened the box. It was a very delicate silver, serpentine chain with a beautiful princess cut diamond pendant hanging from it. "Thank you, Julian. You didn't have to buy something so expensive for me."

"It's my money. If I want to give you something nice I will, okay? And, anyway, I thought I might scare you away if I bought the ring too soon."

I was speechless. What do you say to the 'faunest' man in the room when he starts talking about rings? It was a bit early in our relationship and I wasn't looking for a husband, but the thought was nice. While I was lost in thought, Julian proceeded to get up and walk behind my chair to help me put my necklace on. I guess there was nothing else to be said about the gift. Afterwards, he asked me if it was okay if he read the card when he got home. I thought it was a bit strange and I was a little disappointed because I wanted to see his reaction when he read it, but it was okay.

"I don't know. I've always liked to read my cards in private. Just one of my quirks." I gave him a reassuring smile.

"No explanation needed. Seems a little strange, but to each his own."

During dinner I finally broke down and told him about the young lady that had come to the table before he arrived. We discussed it and he assured me that he wasn't seeing anyone else. As a matter of fact, he was adamant about it and a little angry that someone would step to me like that. So, to avoid it ever happening again, he suggested we meet at his house next time. He thought that would be a little safer because the young lady really could have been some kind of psycho-groupie or worse.

"Don't you think it's about time we took this to the next level anyway?"

He was right. "I agree. I guess it would be nice to have our next tête-à-tête at your place." I was a little apprehensive, but I don't know why. We had to stop meeting at the restaurant eventually. I had to shake my head at myself. It really had been a long time since I dated.

When the day finally arrived, I drove over to Julian's house. After entering the gate and driving a few blocks, his house was far more beautiful than I had anticipated. As I pulled onto the two-lane, circular drive in front of a huge, beige, stucco mansion, I thought it was just like him not to tell me about his home. Not that it mattered, but it was a pretty fabulous house. Now that I thought about it, he never talked about his money or the things that he had acquired with his newfound wealth, and I had never asked.

Though, I knew I was at the right house, I thought maybe I had my days mixed up because there were six or seven other cars in the driveway. I almost kept driving, but, instead, I got out of my car and walked up to the front door. I barely heard a full chime from the doorbell before Julian opened the door. He had been looking out for me, in the event I got lost or something. As I walked in, we exchanged hellos, he grabbed me by my left hand, kissed me on the cheek and gave me a big hug before closing the door.

I immediately noticed all of the people in the house, so I turned and looked up at him. "It looks like you already have company."

"I knew you were a little nervous about coming over and I didn't want you to feel uncomfortable, so I invited some folks over to hang out."

I smiled. "So we have a house full of chaperones."

"Yep."

Julian took me by the hand and walked me through the house, introducing me to everyone along the way. Then he led me through the kitchen and out the back door. We sat by the pool and had dinner by candlelight.

This was my opportunity to be honest with him. "Julian, I think you're absolutely wonderful, but I don't know if I'm ready for a relationship yet. I think we have a really good friendship going and I want to, you know, do this for a while."

Julian raised his eyebrows. "So, when can we become more than friends? Is there anything that I can do to change your mind?"

"Right now, I just don't…I'm not ready to date. Things get complicated, sex and everything, you know. And since I threw that out there, I might as well tell you that I'm celibate. So…"

There was no room for discussion when it came to sex. I think Julian was a little disappointed, but it was hard to tell. He had a really sweet, boyish look on his face as he listened to me.

"I understand." He smiled and continued to eat.

"What do you understand?"

"I understand what you just said."

And that was the end of that portion of our conversation. He didn't question me and I didn't question him. We continued to talk into the night. Julian mentioned several parties that he had to attend in the next few months. He wanted me to go with him.

"Uh, uh, I'm not a party person, so I won't be going to a bunch of parties with you. And I'm really not into parties where there might be a lot of drugging, drinking, and stuff going on." I slowly shook my head from side-to-side.

"You read too many tabloids. All entertainers don't drink and do drugs." Julian sat back in his chair and laughed.

I guess he had a point.

"That's cool. I just want to spend time with you. Who knows, maybe one thing or the other will change, but until then I hope we can continue to hang out together." He paused, as if to give me time to respond. "Shelby look, there is one party I really want you to go to with me. I'll buy your outfit, you know, whatever."

"You don't have to do…"

"I know, but I want to. Consider it my way of saying thank you."

I finally conceded, and we made plans to go shopping on Sunday, which was only two days away.

I sat back in my chair, crossed my arms across my chest, and looked down at my watch. "It's getting late and it looks like most of your houseguests have left. I should probably go, too."

A Cheshire cat smile spread across his face. "You don't have to leave. I have plenty of bedrooms here. You're more than welcome to stay."

"Julian, for real?"

"What? I'm trying to be a gentleman."

"I know you are." I stood up.

"Okay then, I guess I'll walk you to the door."

The flurry of activity that had greeted me when I arrived had now ceased. Neither Julian nor I disturbed the quietness as we silently walked through the house to the front door. Once we were outside we stood by the driver side door of my car. I turned and faced him. He was so close I could feel his breath on my face.

"Well, good night, Mr. Brishard."

Grasping my left hand he raised it to his lips and gently kissed it. "I hate to see you go and I can't wait to see you again. I want you."

"Oh…"

Julian leaned over and kissed me on the forehead, and then softly kissed me on the lips. "Good night, Shelby Simone." Then he stepped back. "Let me get the door for you."

After I got into my car. He closed the door for me as I started the car. I watched him in my rearview mirror as he watched me drive away.

As I drove, I chuckled because tonight Julian made his intentions unmistakably clear and, whether I was ready to admit it or not, I wanted the same thing, too. I don't know why I was still a little gun-shy, though. I'm going to have to do a lot of praying. I don't want to mess this up because I sure do like being with him.


Saturday evening my phone rang and it was Julian. "I have a surprise for you. Meet me at my house around 7:30 this evening." Then he hung up before I could say anything.

When I pulled up, Julian was waiting outside. He quickly ushered me out of my car and into his. We rode until we arrived at the beach. Once we were there he spread a blanket on the sand, and then went back to the car and removed a wicker picnic basket from the trunk of his vehicle. As instructed, I sat on the blanket thinking, *I cannot believe this man.* It had been a long time since I had been romanced. He was going to win me over very quickly if he kept doing things like this. He pulled fruit, cheese, crackers, a portable CD player, two wine glasses, and a bottle of wine out of the basket.

Julian handed me a glass of wine, and then poured one for himself. "I want to assure you, I heard everything you said last night, but, for real, I can't get you off my mind. I appreciate you being honest with me because I'm not used to that. This might sound like a line, but you're not like anyone I've ever met."

I attempted to interrupt him, but he pressed his finger against my lips.

"We've only known each other for a little while, but I feel like we have history together. And you know what's strange? I think I'm falling in love with you. I'm not asking you for anything and I'm not trying to put any pressure on you. I just need you to know how I feel."

I sat there wondering where all of this was coming from.

"I just want to share the sunset with you tonight, though. That's all." Then he turned away, took a drink from his glass, and looked out at the ocean as I sat there looking at the side of his face.

I didn't know what was more beautiful, him or the sunset. I took a sip from my glass as I turned away and looked out at the ocean. His words echoed in my mind. "I think I'm falling in love with you…" As I was daydreaming, I felt Julian's hand on my cheek. He turned my face toward his and gently kissed me on the lips. It was really nice. So far, everything about him was nice. When he sat back we looked at each other, and then kissed again. I thought the second kiss was going to last forever—sort of cliché, but that's how it felt. I didn't want it to end. His kiss was strong and sweet. I honestly didn't know if I had ever liked kisses as much as I liked his. Maybe it was just that it had been a long time since the last time I kissed. When it was over neither one of us said a word. I leaned up against him and we watched the sunset.

# Chapter 3

Lately, it seemed like all I did was wait for the next time I would see Julian. I was going on with my day-to-day life, but Julian was always on my mind. I wondered what he was doing, if he was thinking about me, what he was wearing. You know...silly stuff. It was hard to believe almost three months had gone by and I hadn't told any of my friends or family about him. It wasn't that I was keeping my relationship with him a secret; I just wasn't quite ready to share him with anyone else yet. Another strange thing was that he had never been to my condo. That was going to change this weekend because he was going to pick me up for the party. We always spent time at his house, so there had really been no reason for him to come to my place.

I was trying very hard to keep things in perspective. After all, I was the one that said I wasn't ready for a relationship. If I really believed what I had said I wouldn't be thinking about him all the time. One day I even thought: *If I didn't know any better I'd think I was falling in love with that boy*. When I'm with him I feel 'some kind of way.' I really can't put it into words. He doesn't make any unreasonable demands of me. I don't have to make any extra effort to make him happy and we can talk about anything. He's unpretentious. He's warm, generous, caring, and giving. You know…all of the good things that any woman would want, but often gives up when she thinks she has to make a compromise. As much as I wanted to control my feelings I couldn't and I'm sure Julian knew that. And you know what else? He doesn't seem to have a problem telling me how he feels. It has never once crossed my mind that Julian might be 'too good to be true.' I couldn't even imagine him being anything other than what he is.


Party night finally arrived. I stood back and looked at myself in the mirror. I looked good in the black, hand-embroidered, scallop-edged cocktail dress Julian picked out, even though the plunging neckline almost made me feel like I had the dress on backwards. It was more daring than anything I would have picked out for myself. My black, strappy, patent leather, platform Louboutin sandals, also courtesy of Julian, were perfect with my dress. Turning to the left, and then to the right, I checked myself out from the back. I playfully kicked up my heel then struck a pose. When the doorbell rang I unexpectedly began to feel a little nervous. The party would be our coming out date, so to speak.

When I opened the door we both stood back and admired each other. Julian looked good in his black tux.

For a moment, I almost forgot my manners. "Wow, I'm sorry, come in. Welcome to my home."

When he stepped into the foyer he grabbed me by my waist, pulled me close, and kissed me.

"Step back and let me look at you. Girl, you look good. I wouldn't be surprised if somebody tried to steal you from me tonight. Turn around, let me see. Uh, huh." The smile on his face stretched from ear to ear.

"You don't look so bad yourself, sir. Give me a second to grab my purse and I'll be ready to go."

After we made our way back down do his limo, the ride to the party was really nice. We spent most of it holding hands and looking at each other and laughing like high school kids. I was content in the back seat of the car with Julian. I wouldn't have had a problem with riding around town in the car and missing the party all together.

"You look really beautiful tonight."

I laughed at him. "What have I been looking like before now?" I hit him on his leg.

"No, no, that's not what I'm saying. You're always beautiful, but tonight you are exceptionally beautiful."

I took a sip from the glass of wine I was drinking. "You did a good job of cleaning that up. So, tell me, what should I expect tonight?"

"You know, lots of industry folks, groupies, lots of beautiful people. You'll be fine, though."

When we arrived, limousines and expensive cars were everywhere. I began to feel anxious again. Had I made the right decision to come with Julian? I hoped there wouldn't be a lot of craziness. The party was in a huge, white, stucco mansion, located on the top of a hill. I was struck by the number of windows on the house. Because of all of the lighting, the house looked like it was sparkling.

After helping me out of the car, Julian stopped and looked at me. "Are you ready?"

"Ready for what?" His question only managed to make me more nervous, if that was at all possible.

"Why do you look like that? I just mean, everybody's going to be checking you out—because you're gorgeous and because you're with me. There's probably going to be a lot of hating going on, but don't worry, nothing crazy is going to happen. You're definitely going to be the center of attention tonight."

I took a deep breath. "I wasn't trying to hear all of that, but…okay, let's go."

When we walked through the door it was just like Julian said, it seemed like everything, except the music, stopped and all eyes were on us. I could see some people smiling, others whispering, and some nudging each other. There were only a few women, that I noticed, that glared at me. I could only imagine what they were thinking. The attention didn't phase Julian one bit. As we walked through the room, he immediately began to introduce me to everyone he knew. I felt like I was being received well, for the most part.

"Babe, you want a glass of wine? It might help you relax."

I nodded my head.

He grabbed a couple of glasses of wine off the tray of a server that was walking by. While we were standing there, Julian pointed out people he thought I might recognize, and every now and then he would say something funny. He also pointed out two women: one he had dated for a while and the other he had gone out with a couple of times. He felt the need to assure me they were history long before he ever met me. No explanation was needed. I didn't feel threatened. While we were standing there laughing, two music producers walked up and asked me if they could steal Julian away for a few minutes.

"Shelby, sorry, I have to do this." He kissed me on the cheek. "I promise, this won't take long, I'll be right back."

Even though I'm sure it had only been a few minutes, it seemed like Julian had been gone for a while when this guy walked up behind me and whispered in my ear.

"Baby, you look incredible. I didn't see you come in with anybody, so why don't you let me be your date for the rest of the night. Check this out. Let's leave here and go someplace where we can talk and get to know each other better"

"Excuse me?" I turned my head to the right and spoke to him over my shoulder. "Thanks, but no thanks."

When I finally turned around to look at the guy, I was surprised to find a very handsome man with a beautiful smile and smooth, flawless, silky, black skin.

"Girl, look here, we need to leave this party and go someplace where we can talk, where we can get to know each other. If you don't want to drink, that's fine. Let's just get out of here. You're too fine to be standing by yourself at any party."

"I came with Julian Brishard. I'm his new secretary." I was desperate. I just wanted him to leave. In spite of his persistence, he was still a little comical. His advances weren't completely offensive, but there was something about him that rubbed me the wrong way.

He laughed a little bit, stepped back then put his hand over his mouth. "Well go 'head Julian. I didn't think that boy had it in him. I thought everybody he hired was over 50."

I had no idea what he meant by that, but, without missing a beat, he went on.

"Julian very seldom comes to these parties with a date, if he even bothers to come at all. And he brings you, his new secretary. I can't believe my boy didn't tell me about you. You must give good shorthand. Julian doesn't kick it with just anybody, or haven't you been around long enough to know that?"

I didn't immediately respond. Instead, I stood there for a few seconds looking at him. "Do you know Julian very well?"

"Very good guess—for guessing correctly you can have a drink with me at my favorite joint."

Just as I was about to say no thank you for a second time, Julian walked up and kissed me on the cheek.

"I apologize for taking so long." Then he turned and looked at the guy that had been talking with me. "Man, I see you've met Shelby. I hope you weren't sweatin' her? Shelby, this is my best friend, Smokie."

Smokie smiled. "Man, you know me. So this is the friend you were trying to tell me about." Smokie then turned his attention to me. "It was nice meeting you, Shelby. I'm sure I'll be seeing you again soon."

Smokie went on his way and Julian and I held hands and walked to the patio. As the party continued inside, we talked and looked out at the view over the cliff.

"You know what? I'm really enjoying myself, but it's getting kind of late for me. I've made my appearance and, I have to admit, it wasn't as bad as I expected. If you're not ready to go it's okay, you should stay."

He put his arms around me and pulled my back up against his chest. "Come on, girl, stay a little while longer, please? I need to rub a few more elbows and I want to show you off a little more, too."

How could I say no to him? "Okay, Julian, just a little while longer."

We ended up dancing, and then later talking to the hosts for another hour before I left. I made sure to thank them for having such a lovely party and I assured them that Julian and I would have dinner with them soon. I also apologized for leaving so early.

On our way to the car, as we prepared to leave the house, I saw Smokie watching us from across the room.

I felt that strange feeling again. Once we made our way out to the car we stood there as Julian gave me a nice long kiss. I looked at him and thought, *Please don't have multiple personalities or do drugs or be a criminal. Please be for real.*

"Thank you for tonight. I had a nice time." I took my right hand and gently palmed his face and kissed him again before we got into the limo.

As he closed the door, he smiled. "Thanks for coming."

After riding back to my place, he walked me to the door. He stepped inside after I opened the door and immediately grabbed me and kissed me.

"What was that for?"

"I can't get enough of you."

I smiled. "You don't hear me complaining, do you?"

"You want me to talk to Mr. Vestas..."

I put my hand up to his lips. "Good night, Julian." I gave him one last peck on the lips.

"Okay, okay, I hear you." Julian released his hold on me and stepped towards the open door.

He put his hands up over his heart.

"Uh, uh, go on, boy."

Julian playfully sighed. "All right then. I'm going to go home, lonely and sad, by myself. I'll call you tomorrow."

I closed the door and mumbled to myself, *I don't date for years and now this. Could he be the one? I told this man I wasn't ready to date yet, but I'm already in over my head.*

# Chapter 4

It seemed like I had just put my head on the pillow when it was time to get up. That was it, no more parties. It was fun and everything, but I'm so tired I'm nauseous. I had to get up and leave the house for a little while, but I got back as quick as humanly possible. There was one message on the answering machine—Julian. He had called to thank me for the night before and to tell me again how good I looked. He laughed and asked me why I told Smokie I was his secretary. Before he hung up, he said he knew I was tired because he was too, and that he'd call me back later, if I didn't call him first. I guess it never occurred to him to call my cell phone.

The next time I woke up it was going on 5 o'clock in the evening and I really hadn't accomplished a thing, besides getting some well needed sleep. I guess I was sleepier than I thought because I never heard the phone ring. I had three messages: one from Tracie, I forgot I had told her and Kyomi I would hang out with them, and, of course, one from Kyomi. The last message was a pleasant surprise. It was Julian again. I couldn't hang out with him because I hadn't spent a weekend with my friends in weeks. They were going to start thinking that I was doing something I didn't want them to know about. I called Tracie and Kyomi back first, and then I called Julian.

There was no answer when I called Tracie, so common sense told me she was probably already at Kyomi's house. I was right.

I didn't want to give Kyomi a chance to say a word, so I spoke quickly. "Hi, where are we going today?"

"You must have had a hot date because Tracie and I have been blowing up your cell phone and your house phone."

Bossy and nosey, that would be Kyomi.

"Yes, ma'am, you are correct. I did have a hot date."

"Are you serious, with who? Is it anybody we know?"

"You know him well—my bed. I was sleep"

We both laughed. Eventually we decided to ride out to Landmark Park and do some people watching. There was some sort of festival going on, so, if nothing else, the people watching would be interesting. I was told I was driving because I wasn't in place when they called me. I agreed to meet them at Kyomi's apartment. As soon as I hung up the phone I called Julian.

"Hello."

"Hey, girl. What's going on with you?"

"I got your messages and you are most certainly welcome. What were you doing when I called?"

"Sitting here thinking about you."

I blushed. "Besides that?"

"I'm all partied out, so I thought I'd spend some time at home, alone, unless you want to come over?"

"As nice as that sounds, I have to spend some time with my friends today. What would you and I be doing besides sitting around your house?"

"I can think of plenty of things, but even if that was all we did that would be fine with me."

"Let's do something the end of next week. By then we might come up with something fun to do."

"Well, I don't know about waiting until the end of the week, but my invitation is still open. If you get tired of hanging out with your girls just come on over. You know you don't have to call."

"Okay, I don't think so, but we'll see."

I hated to hang up the phone, but I did.


As I was driving to Kyomi's, I knew that now would be a good time to tell them about Julian. He and I have been seeing each other for almost four months. It was time. I needed to introduce him to my family and friends because, who was I kidding, it wasn't like I was going to end the relationship anytime soon. When I finally arrived at Kyomi's she and Tracie immediately lit in on me for being so slow. I've suffered from slowness since childhood. In my early twenties I came to the conclusion it was chronic, though it does go into remission from time to time. If someone were to ask me if I was a punctual person, I'd have to say, *No, but I am consistent*—consistently late.

The ladies quickly piled into my car and we headed for the park. From the back seat, Kyomi immediately started in on me and it was apparent that she wasn't going to be satisfied until she knew why I was so tired.

"So, again, tell me about this hot date, and don't be trying to play us and tell us you were just sleeping."

"Okay, I went out last night and stayed out too late."

Tracie sat almost side-saddle in the front passenger seat. "So, where did you go?"

I stared straight ahead as I drove. "I went to a party out on the Point."

Kyomi leaned forward between the seats. "And you didn't take us? What's up with that? Who do you know up there?"

I didn't want to tell them about Julian while I was driving because I wanted to see the expressions on their faces. The next few minutes were filled with question after question: whose house was it; what did you wear; how did you get invited; who was there; what did the house look like; and, finally, the big question, who did you go with? I didn't answer the last question. Fortunately, I saw a parking space and thought, *Okay, find a nice comfortable bench where we can sit and talk, and then tell them about Julian.*

"Y'all ask too many questions. Can I please park the car?"

They looked at each other and then at me.

"That's okay, before we leave this park today, you're gonna' tell us who you went to that party with." Kyomi sat back in her seat as she and Tracie cracked up.

Tracie held her finger up to her lips and looked at Kyomi. "Shh, don't say anything else right now; she's trying to park the car."

We laughed as we exited the car and walked toward the park.

We went straight to the first ice cream vendor we saw. In spite of trying not to eat a lot, we often lost total control when it came to food. As soon as we bought our ice cream, I suggested we find a bench to sit down and eat.

I didn't know how to tell them about Julian, so I just started talking. "I met somebody."

Kyomi immediately stopped eating. "Where, while you were at the party?"

"No, the person I met invited me to the party. His name is Julian—Julian Brishard."

Before I could get another word out Tracie interrupted. "Isn't there a singer name Julian Brishard or Jules Brishard or something like that?"

I looked at both of them. "Yeah…that's him. I met him at the Bistro after work one day."

They both started screaming.

"Girl, stop playing with us. You went out with Jules Brishard?" Kyomi could barely contain herself. "He is too fine."

Tracie acted like she was falling off the bench. "I don't believe you. You went out with him, for real? I mean, how? It's just like you to keep something like this secret."

I smiled. "Let's see, he's a perfect gentleman and he's a nice guy. Oh, and he smells really good."

I thought we all were going to hyperventilate from laughing so hard. I was glad they weren't mad at me for not telling them sooner.

Kyomi composed herself for a moment. "Forget all of that silly stuff. How did you manage to go out on a date with somebody like him?"

I took a deep breath. "Well, the party wasn't actually our first date." I winced and shrugged my shoulders. "I've been seeing him for about four months."

They both sat there and looked at me.

"You've been seeing him for four months? You mean seeing him like dating him seeing him?" Kyomi's tone changed.

"Uh, yeah, but no. We're just friends."

"Y'all are just friends. So, why the big secret, I thought we were your girls?"

"Honestly, I don't think either of you should be mad because you are my friends, my best friends. I didn't tell you about him at first because I really thought he and I would have a couple of dinners, a few laughs, and that would be it, but one day he told me he wanted more. With my divorce and everything, you both know I wasn't ready to get involved with anyone.

Things with Julian started off fun, but now it's a little more than just fun, even though I told him I just wanted to be friends. I'm still kind of overwhelmed by the whole thing. I thought about telling y'all about him a few times, but then I thought, 'Am I dating Julian Brishard? This is crazy. What does he want with me?' Then it seemed silly not to say anything about him. I'm telling you now because, well, it would be ridiculous not to."

I sat there quietly looking at both of them, waiting for one of them to say something, anything. For a minute, they both just sat there looking back at me, dumbfounded.

Kyomi was the first to say something. "Are you crazy? I mean, I know you're not, but you act like we want to know every lurid detail of your little romance. Give me a break. I'm hurt because we hadn't seen very much of you lately and we didn't know what was going on with you. Well, that's how I felt, anyway."

"That pretty much sums it up for me too. I just didn't know what was happening with you. Even in the worst of times during your marriage we saw you just about every day, so, for the last couple of months, for you to withdraw from us was kind of weird for me because I didn't know what I could do to help you. I thought you were grieving over the divorce or something." Tracie turned and looked at Kyomi.

"Oh, please…what would she have been grieving over, losing someone who never loved her in the first place? Tracie, sometimes you just make me sick being so melodramatic." Kyomi threw her hand up in the air and turned her head. "You know what? Let me shut up because I'm really getting ready to lose it."

Surprisingly, Tracie responded before I could get a word out. "Yeah, yeah, you're right, you do need to shut up before I have to jump down your throat for saying something you don't have any business saying."

I don't often see Tracie upset, but when I do, it's usually over something Kyomi has said or done. I politely interrupted them.

"Ladies, the subject at hand is my new friend and not whether or not Tracie is a drama queen because she is, but that's a whole 'nother story. To make it up to you guys, I'll just introduce y'all to Julian, how about that?"

"When?" Kyomi looked over at Tracie.

"He's a really busy man, so I don't know when he's going to be free. I'll call him, but I already kind of know that you might have to wait until the end of the week. That's when we had planned on seeing each other."

"Fine, do what you need to do and we might forgive you." Kyomi twisted her lips to one side and turned her head.

We spent the rest of the afternoon at the park laughing and talking about anything other than Julian. I don't know why I was so worried about telling them about him. Well, maybe it had something to do with thinking that I was in love with someone that I hadn't known long. Before we went home we stopped at Wing Wang's, our favorite Chinese restaurant, and had dinner.

When I finally got home I didn't even bother sitting down, I went straight to the telephone and called Julian. There was no answer, so I left a message for him to call me when he got in. It was about 10:15 p.m. In his world that was still relatively early, but it was unusual for absolutely nobody to answer his phone. Someone was always at his house. I filled the bathtub with hot water, poured in a little bath oil, lit a couple of scented candles, and laid out my blue, silk nightie. By the time I got into the tub it was 10:45. It felt good to unwind from the day's activities. Being with Tracie and Kyomi always wore me out.

Just as I was dozing off the telephone rang. It was Julian.

"Hey girl, I didn't wake you up did I? I got your message, so I'm returning your call. I feel like I haven't talked to you all day. The least that I could do is call to say good night."

"Hi Julian."

He laughed. "Hi Shelby."

We both laughed.

"Boy, you didn't even give me time to say hi or anything. What are you doing so full of energy at..." I glanced at the clock. "...11:15?" I knew that wasn't late for him, but he was talking like it was the middle of the afternoon.

"I did a lot of promotional stuff today, so I'm still a little hyped. Once I sit down and relax I'll be all right. What were you doing when I called? Were you asleep?"

I didn't want to be a tease, even though I knew that was how it was going to sound. "I'm taking a candle lit bath."

For a couple of seconds there was silence then, with what I was sure was great restraint, Julian responded. "Candlelight bath, huh. Would it be forward of me to say I wish I was there?"

I thought, what the heck, tease him a little bit. "Now, what would you be doing if you were here?"

He paused. I guess he was trying to place his words very carefully. "I'd wait for you to finish your bath then I'd give you a full body massage, and then I'd just hold you all night long."

He's such a liar. I'm sure he'd be trying to get in the tub with me or he'd be waiting for me to get out, so he could try to have sex with me or something. I didn't say that to him, though.

"Oh, that sounds nice. Let me change the subject for a minute. I want you to meet my two best friends. Will you be home at all tomorrow evening?"

He laughed. I guess he thought we were going to get all into the bath scene. Shame on me if we had started talking about having sex, the next thing you know we would have been doing it all over the place, and I really didn't want things to go down like that.

"I would be glad to meet some of your friends. You should bring them over after 7:00 p.m. At some point tomorrow I was probably going to break down and ask you to come over."

We stayed on the phone for about an hour. By the time we finished talking I had gotten out of the tub, put on my nightie and was lying across the bed.

"It's getting late, Shelby. You ready for that back rub yet?"

I smiled. "You sound a little tired. I'll take a rain check."

"You're too much."

We said good night, but not before he made me give him a good night kiss over the phone. He said it would help him sleep easier. He's so silly.

# Chapter 5

Monday morning is always the same. I never want to get up for work, so I laid in bed for a few extra minutes thinking about how great my weekend was. I love my friends and I really want them to like Julian. I don't know why I spent so much energy worrying about the whole thing. Looking back on it, it was stupid. After I finally got up, I showered, got dressed, and quickly left the house and hopped in my car. As I drove to work I thought about the school day that lie ahead. I hoped for an uneventful but productive day.

Each day as a high school social worker brings new challenges. Because of the unpredictability of the job, one morning I could be talking with a student that had been arrested the day before, mid-day I could be dealing with one who's threatening to commit suicide, and having issues with at least one student a day with behavioral or emotional disabilities is a given. Some days I spend more time talking with parents and other institutions than I do with the students. At the end of the day, it's a great job because it's so rewarding. I couldn't imagine doing anything else. The fourteen to eighteen year olds that are sent to me when they're too much trouble to keep in a traditional classroom setting, but not enough trouble to be expelled from school, make my job very interesting. The biggest reward is when the kids begin to trust me and I'm able to forge a friendship with them. I have the cards, wedding invitations, birth announcements, and pictures to prove it. After they graduate and go on with their lives they remember the administrators and teachers who really cared enough to help them.

I was sure the day would be just as lively as every other workday. In addition to the actual work that I do, kids drop by my office throughout the day to say hi or to talk about the things going on in their lives. Most of the time they just want someone to listen to them, but on the rare occasion that my opinion is requested, I give it— honestly, openly, and tactfully. I guess that's why they keep coming back. I think it's also helpful that I'm not quite old enough to be considered a threat yet. I'm still a little cool.

After arriving and getting acclimated to the day, I could barely concentrate because my mind kept wandering back to the fact that Kyomi and Tracie were finally going to meet Julian. I had it all figured out. We could meet at my place then ride over to Julian's to have dinner, and then, afterwards, sit and talk. First, I had to call Julian. I wanted to remind him to let Miss Gladys, his cook, know we were coming over for dinner. She cooks for him a few days a week and at special request (sort of like this last minute thing).

Miss Gladys has to be about 70 years old, and Julian just loves her to death. He has another woman, not quite as old as Miss Gladys, working for him too. She comes in three days a week to clean his house. He pays them all very well and he treats them like they're his grandmothers. He also has a driver that picks them up for work, and then takes them home when they're finished. Now, I ask you, how could I not love a man that is that thoughtful? I'm sure the way he treats them has a lot to do with him being raised by his mother and his grandmother. He hasn't said a whole lot to me about them, except he's sure they're going to like me and I'm going to like them. I've been told they know all about me, though.

When I finally caught up with Julian I could almost hear him smiling through the phone.

"Hey, boy."

"Hey, girl."

"I'm just calling to remind you that there's just going to be the four of us for dinner, so that y'all can get to know each other without any distractions?

"Of course, I want your friends to feel at home tonight. So, it'll just be us."

"Thank you. You are the best."

"Best what?"

"The best guy ever. If I didn't know any better I'd think you were trying to put me on the spot or something."

"I have to. Things change very quickly in life. I always need to know my place."

I smiled, but remained silent.

"You still there?"

"Uh, huh, I'm still here. Not to worry, you're in a good place with me, Mr. Brishard."

"Okay, that's good to know."

"Well, I better get back to work. I'll see you tonight."

"Absolutely."

After hanging up the phone, I thought about Julian's friend, Smokie. Maybe some time in the near future my friends could meet him, but I didn't think it would be comfortable, for all involved, if Smokie was there. Just from the one time I talked with him, I can tell he can be a bit much to deal with. Apparently, even though he and Julian are best friends, Julian knew his friend could be something to deal with, too. He didn't mention inviting Smokie and I know he knew what I meant when I said just the four of us and no distractions.

It seemed like the day was never going to end, but it did. Before going home I called Kyomi and reminded her to go by and pick up Tracie, and to meet me at my place at 6:30. Of course, there was a last minute crisis at work that had to be resolved and, as if that wasn't enough, there was an accident on the way home that held traffic up for about twenty minutes. All of this extra stuff only took about 45 minutes or so, but it felt like hours.

By the time I pulled into my parking lot I was really nervous. You'd have thought I was getting ready to take my mom and dad to meet Julian. As I parked my car, it occurred to me that Kyomi and Tracie might not like Julian. Well, the idea that he willingly snuck around with me might not make such a favorable impression. And if they don't like him, then what? I don't know why they wouldn't, but it could happen. What if he doesn't like them?

As I walked into the house I glanced at the answering machine—no messages. That was a good sign. I rushed into my bedroom and changed clothes. No sooner had I changed then the doorbell rang. I knew it was Kyomi and Tracie, so I grabbed my purse as I headed for the door. There was really no reason for them to come in and get comfortable because, for a change, I was ready to go.

Surprise registered on their faces as I opened the door. "Hi, ladies."

They greeted me simultaneously, as if singing the chorus to a favorite song. "Hey, girl."

Kyomi looped her arm through mine as I locked the door. "I am absolutely shocked that you're ready."

I smiled and looked at her. "Of course I'm ready. Why wouldn't I be?"

"Let's just go." Tracie laughed.

We laughed and talked for the entire fifteen minutes we were in the car on the way to Julian's. As we exited the interstate, and then entered the gated community, Tracie leaned in between the front seats from the backseat and began looking back and forth at the homes that lined the street.

"I can't believe I'm actually going to get to see the inside of one of these houses. Apparently, all of these years I was correct to assume entertainers, professional athletes, and CEO types lived in the area."

As we approached Julian's driveway Kyomi unknowingly pointed at his house.

"Ooh, look at that one right there, a Mercedes convertible and a Range Rover. How much driving can one person do? Y'all know I'm not into cars, but I would love to just sit in that Mercedes with my shades on and the top down." Then she sat back and laughed.

I put on my turn signal and, because Kyomi was sitting in the front seat, she almost broke my arm and my eardrum when she screamed and hit me.

"Ahh, I can't believe this. Is this his house?" Then she calmed down for a second. "We might be under dressed."

I shook my head from side-to-side. "You're fine."

As we made our way to the front door, Tracie joked around and pushed ahead of us. "Girl, let me ring the doorbell. I've never rang a doorbell at a house like this before. I bet it sounds just like in the movies."

As she put her finger on the buzzer, Julian opened the door. He had on a pair of jeans and a loose fitting, white cotton shirt, with the top two buttons unbuttoned. He looked so good I wanted to push my friends out of the way and grab him by his collar and kiss him. Instead, he stepped aside and welcomed us in. As I walked in he gently grabbed me by my waist and kissed me on my right cheek. After kissing me he closed the door and extended his hand.

As Tracie shook his hand he pulled her over and gave her a quick hug. It's good to finally meet you."

Kyomi, as to be expected, was her typical self. "I don't hug strangers."

We all laughed.

"I don't either. Good to meet you, stranger." He hugged her anyway.

Julian grabbed me by the hand and led us into the kitchen. I looked back at the girls as we began walking through the house. They were holding hands, mocking me and Julian. I smiled and mouthed to them to stop being bad. When we arrived in the kitchen Julian stopped and looked around.

"Ladies, you're going to have to serve yourselves. Miss Gladys has gone home for the night."

Tracie playfully looked around as if she was disgusted. "You mean you don't have anyone on staff here to take care of us?"

Julian nodded his head. "Oh, well, actually, other than Miss Gladys, I have an all male staff. When I have beautiful women in my home I confine them to their quarters."

I laughed and shook my head at both of them. "Is this any indication of how it's going to be all night?"

Again, everyone chuckled then Julian gave us directions to the bathroom located between the kitchen and the dining room, so we could go wash our hands, if we were so incline. We quickly came back to fix our plates then headed for the dining room. Miss Gladys had outdone herself. She had prepared curry chicken and rice, Italian stuffed squash, and steamed broccoli. For dessert we had key lime parfaits with Oreo cookie crumbs.

"So, Julian, Ms. Gladys sounds like she might be an older black woman?" Kyomi put a fork full of food into her mouth after she spoke.

"She is."

"Well, she didn't forget the rice, but where are the collard greens and pig feet, or do you not get down like that?"

"You know it's got to be about eating good, healthy food. I mean, we just don't do a lot of slave food around here. They didn't eat the healthiest meals in the world. Know what I mean?"

We all laughed. As a matter of fact, we laughed throughout dinner. It was great. When we finished, Julian offered to clean off the table and serve dessert. Kyomi and Tracie protested and insisted on doing it themselves, but Julian won out.

"Y'all have got to be kidding, right? You're guests in my home. Sit back and relax. After tonight you'll be like family and you won't get this kind of service ever again. Take advantage of it while you can." Then he turned and looked at me. "Shelby, would you please help me carry the dishes to the kitchen?"

"So, I guess that means I'm not a guest."

Julian shook his head. "Uh, uh, sorry, kiddo."

I really didn't mind. I grabbed some of the dishes off the table and hurriedly followed behind him as he exited the room. While I was rinsing the dishes off and putting them in the dishwasher, Julian stood behind me and kissed me on the back of my neck.

I turned around to face him. "Come on, boy, we have people in the other room, and they're waiting for their dessert."

"I know, but I'm trying to get my dessert, right here, right now."

When he kissed me all I could think about was how weak I was getting. Julian was wearing me down, in more ways than one. Because of his weight, I lost my footing and fell up against the open dishwasher door, knocking some of the dishes around in the rack.

Kyomi hollered from the other room. "Y'all okay in there? Do you need some help?"

Julian hollered back. "No, we have everything under control. We're trying to get dessert." Squinting his eyes, he looked at me, smiled, and gave me another peck on the lips.

We had dessert in Julian's entertainment room and laughed and talked until a little after 11 o'clock. It was good to see my two best friends getting along so well with my new friend. At one point during the conversation I got up and left the room to step out on the patio. As I walked toward the pool I stared at the reflection of the moon in the water. I closed my eyes for just a second and took in the coolness of the breeze. I was content. I shook my head, smiled to myself, and turned around and went back into the house. As I approached the entertainment room I could hear Kyomi talking. Apparently, they weren't talking about the same thing they were talking about when I left the room, so I paused to listen to what was being said.

I could vaguely make out a word here and there. It sounded like Kyomi was telling Julian they loved me …that I had been through a whole lot in the last few years…that I deserved to be happy….she could tell that I cared a lot for him…didn't want to see me hurt again…was he going to ask me to marry him? I lowered my head and put my hand up to my mouth. I hadn't seriously considered marrying anybody, so I was a little surprised that she would assume something like that, and then have the nerve to ask him. I was waiting to hear Julian's response when Tracie walked up behind me and almost startled me.

"What'cha doin', Shelby?"

I didn't scream, but that was only because my hand was already covering my mouth. I turned around and hit her on the arm. "You scared me, girl."

"Oh, okay. If you hadn't been creeping, you wouldn't be so scared." Tracie laughed as she walked ahead of me.

I never heard the end of the conversation between Julian and Kyomi. When Tracie and I walked into the room they stopped talking and turned and looked at us. Julian grabbed me by my hand, pulled me over to him, and kissed me on the cheek.

I looked at him. "What was that for?"

"Because I...I wanted to. Is that a problem?"

I looked at him and thought, *Boy, if you only knew*.

We had to go to work the next morning, so now was as good a time as any to ask the ladies if they were ready to leave. Julian held my hand as he walked us out to the car. When we got to the car Kyomi turned around and gave him a really big hug and a kiss on the cheek. Tracie hugged him too. While they were getting in the car, Julian walked around to the driver's side, gently cupped my face with both of his hands, and kissed me on the forehead. As he was opening the driver side door for me he thanked me for a great evening. After getting into the car, I rolled down the window and Julian stuck his head in to talk with Tracie and Kyomi.

"Now that y'all know where I live, don't be strangers."

They both said okay before he stepped away from the car. As I backed out of the driveway, Julian told me to call him when I got home.

During the ride home Kyomi and Tracie couldn't say enough nice things about Julian.

"This is just your first time meeting the man and y'all are acting like y'all really know him." I was happy to hear their comments.

It was kind of ironic, though. After my first evening at the restaurant with Julian I thought I knew him too. When I got home I gave both of my friends their hugs in the parking lot and we agreed to talk the next evening. I went into my condo and headed straight for my bedroom. I got ready for bed, and then called Julian. His phone only rang once before he picked up.

"We made it home safely, Julian, you can go to bed now."

I could tell he was tired. His laugh was softer than usual. "Thanks for calling. I enjoyed your friends tonight. They both seem real nice. I meant what I said, they're welcome here any time."

Before we hung up I tried to get him to tell me what he and the girls had talked about, especially Kyomi, but he wouldn't tell me anything, so I stopped pressing him about it.

Julian seemed to have everything that I thought I wanted in a man: a strong personality, yet really respectful; gentle and attentive, but not demeaning; and I absolutely loved the way he looked at me when I talked to him. I could see in his eyes that the only thing that mattered for that very moment was me. He treated me like the intelligent woman that I know I am and, at the same time, he made me feel sexy and sophisticated. After three years of being verbally and mentally abused, Julian was a breath of fresh air. If he wasn't what I needed, he sure was what I wanted. My mind was made up, I was going to do this thing with Julian, and, as the saying goes, "It's all good."

# Chapter 6

The following morning, at work, I received a call from Julian.

"Shelby Simone, good morning."

"Good morning, Julian Brishard. To what do I owe this pleasure?"

"My people scheduled some promotional events for me and I'm going to have to leave town in an hour and a half. I'll be gone for about two weeks. I won't get to see you for two whole weeks; can you believe that? It's a good thing you came over last night."

I was disappointed, but I understood. It was the nature of the business he was in.

I tried not to sound too whiny. "Two whole weeks, huh? Wow."

"I promise, I'll call you as soon as I can. I know I'm going to have some early mornings and late nights, so I'll try not to call you too late. You know what, though, doggone?"

"What?"

"I'm not even going to be able to get a goodbye kiss. Can you meet me at the airport?"

"I can't. Too much going on at work today."

"I guess you're going to have to give it to me over the phone then."

We did our little kissy-kissy over the phone, and then we hung up. I really didn't care how late it was, as long as he called me. As soon as we hung up I started missing him.

I was really surprised when Thursday evening rolled around and I still hadn't heard from Julian. I was getting kind of worried. As I considered whether or not I should call him, my phone rang. It was almost 8:30 p.m. My heart skipped a beat because I knew it was him. It was a local area code, but not a phone number that I was familiar with.

When I answered the phone I tried not to sound too anxious. "Hello…"

The voice on the other end wasn't Julian's, but it did sound familiar. "Hey, baby, what'cha doin'?"

I responded quickly because I didn't have time for games. "Who is this? You better hurry up and say something because I'm getting ready to hang up." When I heard the deep, throaty laugh I knew who it was. "Smokie?"

He continued to laugh. "If it makes you feel better you can call me Julian, with your sexy black self."

"Did Julian tell you to call me?"

Smokie is definitely the kind of guy that no matter what you say to him you can't hurt his feelings. His ego is too big.

"Shelby, Shelby, Shelby, can't I just call to check on you? Julian is busy and I know you're a little lonely."

I could just imagine him grinning from ear to ear.

"Smokie, is Julian okay, did he tell you to call me? You know what? I'll call him myself."

Smokie wasn't quite finished yet, though. "Look, Julian asked me to call and check on you and I'm doing it. I take my responsibilities to my boy very seriously. If I could, I'd come over there and take care of you. You know, in the past Julian and I have shared everything. I don't see why things should change now."

"Look, I don't have time to play games with you, Smokie. If Julian asked you to check on me then fine, you've done it. If he didn't then I would advise you to lose my number. I'll pretend we never had this conversation, and when you do talk to Julian you have him call me. Good night, Smokie." I would have been amused, but I didn't know if he was serious or joking.

Of course, instead of getting mad, Smokie laughed. "I knew you weren't as quiet as you looked. You got a little fire in you. I love a woman who speaks her mind. You have a good night and sleep tight. I'll talk to you later." He continued laughing as he hung up.

Smokie is a trip. I still didn't hear from Julian until Saturday, after I received a beautiful bouquet of gladiolas.

"I knew I was going to be busy, but I didn't know my schedule was going to be non-stop. Before today, I haven't even been able to take a minute to stop and call you and talk to you like I wanted to..."

"I'm fine. I miss you too. Oh, and thank you for the flowers. They're beautiful."

"So you got them. Good. I'm really sorry. I'm going on and on. I can't wait to get back home to you."

Any anxiety I had been feeling went away the moment I heard him say "I can't wait to get back home to you." I missed him too much to fret over not hearing from him for a few days or receiving a phone call from Smokie. After we ended our call, I did feel the sting of reality slap me in the face, though. My future with Julian would be filled with quite a few sleepless nights.


One of my sisters and two of my brothers were coming to visit. We always had a great time when we got together, but this time I was going to introduce them to Julian. The plan was to have Julian over for dinner their first night in town and afterwards we could hang out at my house, so they could get to know each other. For their second night, I had asked Julian if he would invite a few of his celebrity friends over for a casual get together. Nothing elaborate, just a few folks over to mingle with. As far as I'm concerned, two days of entertainment was going to have to be enough. My job as a gracious hostess would be done.

Because everybody was flying in on Thursday afternoon, I was only going to work half a day, and then on my way to the airport stop by the grocery store to pick up the seafood: crab legs, shrimp, oysters, clams, and grouper fingers. Dinner was going to be simple, seafood with hush puppies and salad. I always had lemonade in my refrigerator, so it we could drink that or water. I figured, if anybody wanted cocktails before, during, or after dinner, I had a couple of bottles of wine in the pantry, but, of course, we could always stop at the liquor store on the way from the airport. Dinner was covered and my plans to pick them up from the airport were in place, so it was just the small matter of getting away from work.

Fortunately, my work day was pretty uneventful. Right before it was time for me to leave, though, one of my favorite students came by my office to hang out. My very first thought was a selfish one, *I hope Sergio isn't having a crisis today because I'm leaving in 30 minutes, no matter what.* Of course, I wasn't going to tell him that.

"Good afternoon, Sergio. What can I do for you today?"

Sergio Stanton is one of the more colorful students at the school, and probably my favorite. He's really intelligent and creative, and has a great sense of humor. I completely understand why so many female students are attracted to him. It's because of that same fantastic personality that I've had to talk with him and his girlfriend, as well as six other 10th through 12th grade female students, thus far this school year. Every single one of the girls was willing to do anything, short of killing each other, to be with him. And then there was the incident with a student teacher. She came to talk with me because her job was in jeopardy. She enjoyed flirting with Sergio and didn't know how to put a stop to it. In spite of all of that, he's still a good kid.

Sergio plopped down in a chair in front of my desk. "Hi, Miss Simone. I haven't been by to talk with you in a while. I wanted to see how you were doing."

"I'm flattered that you've been thinking about me. That's nice of you, Sergio. I'm doing just fine. You guys keep me on my toes, though. Speaking of which, how are you and your girlfriend doing these days?"

"You talking about Mia? We broke up. We're just going to be friends. You know she's leaving for Howard University as soon as she graduates, right? I ain't tryin' to get played. I know how it works. She'll leave here all in love, meet her a knucklehead on campus, and then I'll get one of them Dear John letters talkin' 'bout we can be friends. I think we can skip all that and be friends right now. Don't you agree, Miss Simone?"

I actually thought that was a very mature decision. "Well, Sergio, I feel like you're thinking very realistically. When people go off to college they do make a lot of new friends. How did Mia feel about your decision?"

"She didn't like it. She tried to tell me why we should stay together. Then she started cryin'. What's up with girls cryin' all the time, Miss Simone?"

Men and boys are just alike when it comes to women. They don't have a clue.

"Well, maybe she cares about you, Sergio. You ever thought about that?" I knew he was smart enough to realize that.

"Of course. I care about her too. It ain't like that. I just think it's better to take care of business right now. We'll both be all right. She's going off to college and I got another year in high school. I'm a lot of things, but I ain't stupid and I'm not gone' let nobody play me."

I smiled at him. "I agree, you're not stupid and you've made a very mature decision. I'm sure both of you'll be all right. I just have one question. Why did you break up now, there're still four months left in the school year?"

Sergio rubbed his chin. "Well, I just wanted to be able to mend my broken heart while I still had girls around to help me heal." He grinned as he put his hands over his heart.

I sat there and looked at him for a second. "Go to lunch, young man." I realized his seemingly mature decision had only occurred because he wanted to play the field. "Sir, I hate to end this wonderful conversation, but I have to leave and you really should go and get yourself something to eat. As usual, though, I've enjoyed your visit."

Sergio left my office and I closed up shop and left for the airport.

# *Chapter 7*

I excitedly walked out to my car. I hadn't seen my family in months, so I was a little keyed up about their visit. My oldest sister, Kary, couldn't make this trip. I imagine, something was going on with her husband or her two kids. Kristoff, my oldest brother, who is also married, couldn't come either. My twin brother and sister, Collin and Sharrin, and my youngest brother, Coleman, were the ones coming to visit.

I stopped and picked up the seafood, and then I headed for the airport. When I arrived, their flight had just landed, so I parked my car and walked to the baggage claim area to meet them. Sharrin is kind of bossy, so I was sure she'd be leading the way. When I finally saw them, sure enough, Sharrin was walking ahead of the guys. Collin and Coleman were lagging behind checking out women. Both Collin and Sharrin are in serious relationships, but I think Collin's girlfriend is more serious about the relationship than he is. Coleman, on the other hand, is always in multiple relationships. He has no real girlfriend, that we know of. If you ask him, he'll say that he has a lot of friends that he hangs out with.

We did a group hug before they checked me out to see if I had gained any weight or if anything else about me had changed. As the youngest girl, my family finds it their appointed duty to lovingly assess me, from head to toe. It's an ongoing family joke. Because both my mom and dad were athletic and did a little modeling in their heyday, my siblings think we should look like movie stars at all times. It's pretty superficial, but it keeps us laughing.

They had eaten a little snack on the airplane, so we didn't stop to pick anything up for lunch, but we did make a stop at the liquor store to get something to make real cocktails with, as Sharrin put it. I had plenty at the house to munch on if anyone just had to eat before dinner. I was about to explode trying to keep the secret about Julian coming over—he was finally going to meet my family. It was going to be interesting to see their reactions when they find out I'm dating again. I knew Coleman was going to be especially pleased because he loves rubbing elbows with the beautiful people. If I had to bet, he would probably spend most of the evening discreetly harassing Julian about women, as in the groupies. I have to admit, Coleman is a bit of a man whore.

Once we arrived at my place we spent the better part of the afternoon laughing, and talking about my parents and Kary and Kristoff. I laugh hardest when I'm around my family. We crack on each other like it was going out of style. If Mom and Dad had come we really would have been rolling on the floor because they are truly characters, mostly because my dad thinks he is a comedian and my mother is his biggest fan. Collin and Kristoff have the best sense of humor and the quickest wit out of all of us, and they both can tell a story like nobody's business—sound effects, facial expressions, the whole nine yards. Around 4:30 p.m. I decided I needed to take a nap because I knew it was going to be a long night. Everybody else was crashing anyway, that is, everybody except Coleman, or Coco, as we call him. He had other plans.

"Look, Sis, let me hold your car keys. I'll be back before y'all wake up."

"I am not. I know you and you won't make it back in time for dinner."

"Am I at my sister's house or back home with my mother?"

"Whatever, I'm still not giving you my car keys."

"Girl, you a trip."

He settled for watching TV, but he made me promise I wouldn't keep him confined in my house all weekend. Little did he know.

It was 6 o'clock before I knew it, so I got up and started getting dinner ready. Coco never fell asleep, or else he only slept for a few minutes. He startled me when he came into the kitchen to help out. I swear that boy only thinks about one thing…women.

"So, Shell, do you have any single friends that I can hang out with while I'm here? She can be single, divorced, or separated, it doesn't matter, as long as nobody comes looking for her while we're together."

I looked at him and shook my head. "I have no single friends that you would be interested in or that would be interested in you."

Coco's enormous ego only allows him to believe that every woman he meets will fall in love with him sooner or later. What's scary is a lot of them do.

I had lost track of time, so when the doorbell rang it caught me off guard. "Don't anybody move. I'll get the door."

I wanted Julian to make a grand entrance, even though he didn't know that was what he was about to do.

"Uhm, you don't have to shout. This is your house, so I don't think any of us were going to rush to the door. And who's coming over right at dinnertime, anyway?" Coco walked behind me and leaned against the kitchen doorframe.

When I opened the door I gave Julian a peck on the lips, grabbed his hand, and escorted him into the living room.

Arm in arm, I proudly entered the room with my guest. "Hey, everybody, I have someone that I want you to meet."

When Sharrin turned around her mouth literally fell open. "Anybody ever tell you, you look just like…"

I smiled. "Julian, this is my sister Sharrin and my brothers Coleman and Collin. Guys this is my…" I stopped and turned to look at Julian. "What are you to me?"

Julian looked at me then looked at my family. "I'm your friend, I think."

"Okay, this is my friend Julian Brishard."

Sharrin, cool as a cucumber, got up and walked over to us and extended her hand, while looking at me. "Shell, it's just like you not to tell anyone that you're dating. Even though you know good and well this is the kind of thing you should tell your sister." She then turned her attention to Julian. "It's not only a pleasure to meet you, but as you may have noticed, it's a surprise, as well. Our sister not only neglected to tell us someone was joining us for dinner, but she also never bothered to tell us that she had been seeing anyone … and look who walks through the door, you, Julian Brishard. It's a pleasure to meet you."

Collin hustled up behind her. "Nice to meet you, man. How'd you have time to meet my sister with all of those fine women in your videos? You gonna' have to hook a brother up?"

Julian laughed. "Your sister ain't so bad. It's good to finally meet some of Shelby's family. She didn't tell me I was going to be part of a scene right out of *Guess Who's Coming to Dinner*."

"Okay, then, good people, I say let's have dinner. If y'all will have a seat, I'll be glad to bring the food to the table. Sharrin, can you come help me?" I grabbed her by the hand to lead her into the kitchen.

Sharrin excused herself and followed me, as the guys headed for the dining room. When we finally sat down and started eating, it was great. Of course, it's pretty difficult to ruin seafood when all you're doing is steaming, frying, and broiling. After dinner we sat in the living room and had a few drinks and talked. Collin had already made his intentions known, now it was Coco's turn.

"Julian, man, when can you introduce us to some of those ladies in your videos? We're leaving Sunday night, so I have to move fast."

"Do you need to meet them before tomorrow?" Laughing, Julian looked over at me. "Oh, apparently Shelby also didn't tell you that you'd be hanging out at my spot tomorrow night."

Sharrin looked at me. "Can we please agree, no more surprises, Shell."

I made a face at her. "Okay, no more surprises, I promise." I looked at Julian. "Can you believe this? I can't even be nice to these people." I plopped down on the couch next to him and grabbed his hand, and rested my hand on his thigh.

"Well, I suggest y'all bring a change of clothes because I don't think any of you are  going to want to drive back to Shelby's place after partying all night."

And that was how dinner ended, everyone full, satisfied, and anxious for the next night. I didn't let on that I was more surprised than my siblings. Julian and I had talked about the party, but he never mentioned spending the night. I guess I was going to be spending the night at Julian's house, too. There would be a house full of people, in addition to my sister and both of my brothers, so it was cool.

The next morning my siblings and I hung around my place and watched talk shows as we ate breakfast. By mid-afternoon we were dressed and ready to go out for lunch, and then, afterwards, a little shopping. Since we were going to the mall we decided to have lunch there. After lunch Sharrin and I were going to go do our thing and the brothers were going to go and do theirs.

"Hey, y'all, the party is going to be pretty casual, so don't feel like you have to go out and spend crazy money on an outfit." I could tell by the way everyone was looking at me that none of them were listening to a word I was saying.

"Say what you want, Sis, I'm trying to look good tonight. "Coco rubbed his chin and started walking away. "Meet you right back here in a couple of hours."

I already knew what I was going to wear. I just had to buy it. A week or so before I had seen a black mini-skirt and a black, long sleeved, mock turtleneck, and some black ankle boots. I already had the perfect black leather belt that would pull it all together. I knew exactly where I needed to go, so Sharrin and I headed one way and the guys headed another. It didn't take Sharrin long to find what she wanted to wear. She settled on a leopard print top and a little brown spandex mini-skirt.

"What do you think, Shell? Be honest because I want to look good tonight." She rolled her eyes as she turned from side-to-side looking at her reflection in the mirror. "No, really, I want to look sexy. Do I?"

I looked at her with my head tilted and my lips pursed. "You know what I think. It's cute and it's too short, but since I know that's not what you want to hear…yeah, it looks good. And, of course, it's very sexy."

Satisfied, Sharrin turned away and simultaneously looked in the mirror at her butt one last time. She smiled and raised her eyebrows at me when she made eye contact with my reflection.

I rolled my eyes, and then turned my head and started laughing. "Girl, you're crazy." I knew she had already decided to get the outfit before she came out of the dressing room. She just wanted to hear me say she looked good in it.

After Sharrin bought her skirt and blouse, we went to a shoe store, and then we met up with the guys. Coco had gotten a pair of black jeans and a yellow mock, polo turtleneck with a black stripe around the chest. He was going to wear it with his black Timberland boots. Collin bought a long sleeve, purple DKNY shirt to wear with a pair of black slacks and a pair of black, double-buckle Kenneth Cole ankle boots he brought with him. After we looked over each other's purchases we headed home. Once we arrived at my house we talked while they waited for me to pack an overnight bag. By the time I finished it was going on 6 o'clock. We then piled into my car and I drove us over to Julian's place to get ready for the party.

As we approached the gated community, Coco started laughing. "Oh, man, that's what I'm talkin' 'bout. We ain't got to worry about no riff-raff crashing the party."

I looked over my shoulder at him. "Coco, my dear brother, I believe you are the riff-raff."

We laughed as we turned onto Julian's driveway.

"Sis, stop playin'. This can't be Julian's house. His joint is tight."

We went through the gate to the back of the house. I could see the Range Rover parked in the garage, so Julian must have driven his other car. We got out of the car and went in the house through the kitchen. I introduced everybody to Miss Gladys, who was on her way home. Mr. Vestas was in his apartment over the garage, waiting to take her home.

Miss Gladys hugged my siblings like she had known them for years. "Y'all are some nice looking children. Now, y'all young people relax and make yourselves at home. Jules will be home in a little while. Shelby, the hors d'oeurves are set up in that big ole walk-in cooler over there." Miss Gladys pointed like there was a chance I might not know where the walk-in cooler was. "If I'm not mistaken, two or three servers will be showing up in a little while. The only thing they'll need to do is uncover the platters when you're ready to start the party.

The hors d'oeurves that have to warmed can be put in the oven. You can show the servers where everything is, okay?"

"Yes, ma'am. Thank you, Miss Gladys. I'll take care of it."

When Coco walked over to Miss Gladys I wasn't sure what he was going to do.

"So, you mean, you're not going to stay for the party, Miss Gladys?"

She laughed heartily as she patted him on the back. "Oh, Lord have mercy. The music is going to be too loud and it's going to be too many people in the house. That's for you young people. I'm going home to get some rest, so I can try and come back here tomorrow." She turned around one last time. "Oh, Jules said to tell you to put your things away in whatever bedroom you wanted to use. You young ladies are going to share a room, right?"

Sharrin cut her eyes at me and smiled.

"Oh, yes, ma'am. Of course." It was obvious Sharrin wasn't going to respond.

Miss Gladys looked at both of us. "Aw'right then. Have a good night, now."

"Yes, ma'am." Coco smiled and turned around and poked his tongue out at us as he walked Miss Gladys out the back door.

"He's such a pervert. He thinks he can sweet talk any woman." Sharrin grabbed her bag and looked at me. "Okay, direct us to our rooms."

Sharrin and I went upstairs and picked a room at the opposite end of the hall from Julian's room. It was the only bedroom that had two full beds. Coco and Collin got separate rooms closer to Julian's. I could only imagine what Coco's plans were. Once we settled in and unpacked, I took everyone on a quick tour of the house. Because we were upstairs, we started with Julian's bedroom. Coco was surprised to find one entire wall of the room mirrored.

"When I met brother-man I thought he was kind of conservative, but I don't know. The mirrors all over the place kind of making me think something different now. What are all them mirrors for, Sis?"

I started laughing. "Coco, some people just appreciate the decorative quality of mirrors. Thank you very much." Crazy thing was, I had never seen the mirrors before. This was my first time in Julian's bedroom.

Our laughter filled the air as we exited the room. I took one last look inside the room before I closed the door behind me.

# Chapter 8

After touring the entire house, we sat in the entertainment room and waited for Julian to arrive. Collin had been pretty quiet, so it was about time for him to say something

"Obviously, Julian can blow. All we have to do is look at the size of his house and listen to the radio to know that he can make money. Does he have anything around that's not electronically enhanced?"

I was insulted because Collin was insinuating Julian was one of the many professional lip synching performers that we so often hear on the radio, who couldn't perform live in concert no matter how much money you paid them. I had yet to hear Julian in concert and had honestly never thought about it before now, but he was definitely not shy about singing to me. So I had to come to his defense.

"Collin, come on. You don't really think Julian can't sing? You just said yourself he can blow. You hear him on the radio all the time. He sings to me a lot, so let me assure you, he can 'sang.'"

Sharrin stood up and walked across the room towards Julian's CD collection. "I wouldn't care if the brother couldn't sing a note. He could just stand in the room and never open his mouth, as far as I'm concerned. Collin, have you ever looked at him? The man is *'faune.'* If he can't sing, shame on him."

Realizing I was a little offended, Collin tried to clear up the misunderstanding. "Look, I know he can sing. I just wanted to hear his vocals, a little a cappella is all I'm talkin' about."

I calmed down a bit. "Oh, then that's what you should have said. I thought you were suggesting Julian couldn't sing. Okay, so, the answer to your original question is yes, he can sing."

"Girl, you losing it. You 'bout to catch up with Sharrin." Coco looked at me with his lips twisted to one side of his face.

We all looked at him and laughed.

When Julian finally arrived it was about 8:45. We were still sitting in the entertainment room listening to music and to Coco talk trash about how hard he was going to party. We also had to hear what he was going to tell his boys when he got back home. He knew they were going to be jealous when they heard about the party.

Coco got up, walked over to me, and pulled me up from my seat and hugged me. "Thank you for being my favorite sister."

I pushed him away. "Coco, you're just saying that because you're hanging out with Julian. I don't know what to think about your funky, fake gratitude."

"You know what I mean, this is more than any of us expected. This is going to be mad fun. You know, hanging out with celebrities and everything." He laughed and tried to kiss me on the cheek. "Who would have thought that our little sister was dating a celebrity, and one so large?"

I looked at him and pushed him away from me once more. "I think you just insulted me again, but I'm not sure. You might want to stop while you're ahead, before I have to smack you." I mushed him in his face and sat back down.

I could hear Julian shouting through the house. "Shelby and family, where are you? Make some noise so I can find you."

I left the room to meet him. When I found him he was coming down the hall, so I stopped him and threw my arms around his neck and gave him a kiss.

He put his hands on my hips. "I could get used to this, you know. Give me one more."

We kissed again, as Coco rounded the corner looking for us.

"Okay, you two, there's plenty of time for that. We're only in town for the weekend, so, please, let's try not to be rude to the guests."

He and Julian greeted each other with a handshake and a shoulder bump, and then we walked back to the entertainment room where Collin and Sharrin were waiting.

Collin stood up and shook Julian's hand. "So, who's coming to the party tonight, man?"

"Honestly, I'm not really sure. Word gets out that there's something going down and folks show up, people in the business and the full-time groupies. Man, there are people that party every night of the week. I don't know how they do it, but folks get off on house parties, so this place will be packed by 1:00 in the morning."

I looked at him. "1:00? I was hoping things would be wrapped up by then?"

Julian looked at me and laughed. "You thought that, for real? That's so sweet. Baby, a truly good party doesn't even get started until about 1:00, but because y'all are guests in my home I'm starting at 11 o'clock and locking the doors at about 3:00 or 4:00. Your family wants a party, so I'm trying to give them a party." Julian turned his head and looked at Coco and Collin. "And look, if that's not enough, y'all can surely find another party afterwards."

"You have to excuse our sister. She doesn't get out much." Sharrin got up and walked over to change the CD.

"Shut up. I am not going to apologize for not hanging out. There's nothing wrong with it. I just don't do it."

Julian pulled my back up against his chest and put his lips close to my ear. "And that's one of the things I love about you." Then he kissed me on the ear.

"Are the food and drinks going to last that long?" I shrugged my shoulders as I spoke. His kiss tickled.

"Let me tell you something. There is no way that folks will stay at a party if it runs out of food or drinks, so don't even worry about that because Miss Gladys knows the deal. I'm sure, if you check the pantry you'll find more than enough liquor and if you check that walk-in refrigerator you'll find more than enough food. The bartender will be here by 10 o'clock to check the bar, so there's nothing for us to do except relax and enjoy the party."

I already knew I was going to bed at about 1:00. I really had no desire to stay up all night partying.

Coco sang and did a Michael Jackson move. "Oh, yeah, I'm ready to get my dance on right now."


Thirty minutes after midnight the party was going strong. As I walked around I saw a few faces that I recognized, Puff Daddy, or whatever he was calling himself these days, Ne-Yo, and Erykah Badu. I even recognized some dancers from videos that I had seen on different music channels. I thought I saw Raphael Saadiq, who used to sing with Tony! Toni! Tone!. And, if that wasn't enough celebrity sighting for one night, I'm pretty sure the really tall lady I just saw, with the other really tall ladies, was Tyra Banks, and a couple of other models. I've also seen basketball wives and other reality pseudo-celebrities.

People were everywhere, dancing, drinking, and eating. They were even hanging out by the pool. I danced with Julian a few times and told him not to worry about me, to entertain his guests. I'd mingle. One person I hadn't seen all night was Smokie. In a strange way, I sort of missed his presence because, with his special personality, I'm sure he could liven up any party.

I saw Sharrin dancing. She looked good and she looked like she was having a good time, as well. I'm sure she was enjoying all of the attention I knew she was getting. I hadn't seen Collin in a while, but Coco was all over some chick, trying to get with her, I'm sure. She was probably a groupie because she didn't look like anybody I recognized. As an undercover groupie, I continued walking through the rooms looking for entertainers. I was shocked when I glanced around at the staircase and saw Collin coming down the stairs behind some drop-dead gorgeous woman. I looked at him and shook my head. He shrugged his shoulders and mouthed, "What can I say?"

As I watched Collin and his new friend disappear in the crowd, someone walked up behind me and put their arms around my waist.

"What are you doing? Julian might see us."

"What?"

He released his grip and I turned around. "Oh, it's you."

Julian laughed. "Who did you think it was?"

I started laughing, too. "Well, the only people I know here are you and my siblings, and my brothers and I are not that close."

"Girl, you had me worried there for a second." He

pulled me tight up against his chest.

"Yeah, you sounded kind of worried."

"Nah, not for real, I know better. Any other woman, maybe, but you, you wouldn't handle your business like that."

I looked up at him as I held onto his arms. "I wouldn't?"

"Uh, uh." Then he put his finger under my chin and tilted my head up and kissed me softly on the lips. "You wouldn't because you know I love you."

"Oh, okay. Well, I'm getting tired. I think I might call it a night in a little while."

He hugged me a little tighter. "You can't go to bed now, the party is just getting started, girl."

For a few seconds, I continued standing there looking up in his face.

"Okay, okay, I know. Just let me know when you get ready to go upstairs. I want to talk with you before you go to sleep."

"Okay, I think I can do that. I'll find you. I just want to let Sharrin know that she'll have to knock to get in the bedroom because the door will be locked. I'll find you in a few minutes."

I couldn't imagine what he wanted to talk about and I was too tired to try to figure it out. When I found Sharrin, she was talking with some guy, so she introduced us.

"This is my sister, Shelby…"

Before she could get another word out of her mouth, he looked directly in my eyes and extended his hand.

"Man, beauty definitely runs in your family. I'm Dwele. It's a pleasure to meet you, my queen."

"And it's nice meeting you. I like your song, uhm... *What's Not to Love*. It's really nice. I didn't mean to interrupt the two of you, but I need to talk to Sharrin for just one minute. I promise, just one minute." I held up one finger to assure him. Then I looked at Sharrin.

"I just want to let you know that I'm going to bed, so you're going to have to knock hard to get in the room. The door will be locked."

"Are you seriously going to bed now? Girl, hang for a little while longer."

I shook my head. "Uh, uh, I'm really tired. Y'all have a good time. Don't worry about me. You know me." I shook Dwele's hand again and left to look for Julian.

As I made my way through the crowd, I passed a woman that looked vaguely familiar. She was huddled up talking with three other women. Suddenly, it dawned on me where I had seen her before. She was Julian's ex-girlfriends, the one that stared me up and down at that party that I went to with him. I slowed down, but no words were shared between us. After passing her I turned back and smiled to myself, and then I continued to look for Julian. When I found him he was out by the pool playing the gracious host.

"Excuse me."

He excused himself and turned his attention to me. "Just wanted to let you know I'm all partied out."

He grabbed my hand and whispered in my ear. "I'll be there in a minute."

I smiled, nodded my head, and left for upstairs.

Once I was in the room I knew I would fall asleep as soon as my head hit the pillow, and I could hardly wait. With the bedroom door closed, the music wasn't too loud, so I grabbed the remote control and turned on the TV. Instead of taking off my clothes and putting on my pajamas, I stretched out across the bed. I decided to wait until Julian came up, said what he had to say, and then left. Shortly thereafter, I heard a knock at the door and I figured it had to be Julian because there was no way Sharrin was coming to bed this early.

I rolled over and sat up. "Come in."

Julian opened the door. He was holding two glasses of wine and a piece of paper.

I watched as he closed the door behind him. "Where are you going with all of that wine?"

"I brought you a nightcap and I thought it would be rude to let you drink alone." He smiled as he handed me a glass.

I took a quick sip. "You wouldn't be trying to get me drunk to take advantage of me, would you?"

"I hope I wouldn't have to get you drunk to take advantage of you." He laughed out loud.

"Oh…" I took another sip of wine.

Julian also handed me the piece of paper he was holding. "This is my first concert schedule."

I looked it over from top to bottom. He was going to be gone from February to April. His tour was going to start in Atlanta and finish in Phoenix. In between, he would go to Baltimore, New York, Hartford,

Worchester, Pittsburgh, Hampton, Greensboro, Orlando, Miami, Oklahoma City, Denver, Houston, St. Louis, Dallas, Seattle, Sacramento, San Jose, and Los Angeles. We had never been apart for that long, so I got kind of quiet. He must have sensed my apprehension.

"Don't get all emotional on me. I didn't show the schedule to you to make you sad."

"You're going to be away for quite a while." I held up the schedule and looked at him.

He took a drink of wine from his glass and nodded his head. "I know, I was thinking the same thing. That's why I want you to come to my first concert, and then to any of the other concerts that you want to come to after that. Of course, I'll be paying for everything."

I must have been looking at him real crazy because he kept talking.

"Close your mouth. I want you to do what you want to do, but I really want you at my first concert, and then, maybe, one every other week or so. What do you think?"

I hugged him. "That's a great idea. I'd like that." I sat back and looked at him. "You know you spoil me, right?" I bit on my bottom lip.

"No, I don't spoil you. I love you."

Hearing him say he loved me at that moment deserved a kiss. I knew I was in love with him, but I was still a little hesitant to say it back to him. It's crazy, I know, but I wasn't quite ready to say those three words yet. I don't remember sitting my glass down on the nightstand, but I guess I must have. Julian was on top of me kissing me and I could feel his hand going under my shirt. My brain was saying, *Whoa, slow this down. Slow your roll girlfriend, slow your roll,* but my mouth was not cooperating and my body was down for whatever.

Julian whispered in my ear. "Baby, I love you so much. I would go crazy without you for three whole months."

"I would miss you too."

"Can I make love to you, Shelby?" He was rubbing my rubbing my back with one hand and holding the back of my head with the other.

I was going to say yes, I really was, but then the door flew open.

Julian sat up and looked at the intruder. "The party is downstairs, man."

I lie in the bed looking at the ceiling. I never looked over at the door, but I heard a response.

"Oops, sorry, my bad," and then the door closed.

I sat up and we looked at each other in awkward silence.

"You know what? I'm tired, I think I'm going to go to bed now."

"Okay, I guess I should go back downstairs." Julian slowly stood up. "I am having a party, right?" He gave me a peck on the lips before walking to the door. "Good night." As he left the room he turned around one last time. "Make sure you lock the door."

# Chapter 9

The weeks went by quickly. I made sure I was at Julian's first concert to cheer him on. As I listened to the women in the audience scream his name, it didn't take long for me to learn how easy it was to become jealous. They were totally out of control. I knew it was ridiculous, on my part, but it was what it was. In addition, it was dangerous, so Julian arranged for me to have a bodyguard. I felt relatively safe in the event someone in the audience realized I was his lady friend.

With the opening act, the entire concert lasted for 2 ½ hours. At the end of his performance I walked up and gave him two dozen roses. It's amazing how thousands of eyes rolling at the same time feel when they're staring at you. For that moment, it felt very special to be the envy of every woman in the civic center, even if they didn't know that I was really the one he was singing to. I was glad I made it to support him because his show was a hit. Later, all of the reviews would talk about how smooth and sultry he was, how sexy he moved, and how he had every woman in the building in the palm of his hand.

Back stage was crowded. I had to literally push my way through the crowd. Well, my bodyguard had to do a lot of pushing. There were so many people that I almost thought I wasn't going to be able to see him until he got back to the hotel. When I first arrived in Atlanta I went straight to the hotel. Even though I knew Julian was in the hotel somewhere, I didn't try to find him. I didn't want to distract him, but now I was ready to see him. When I finally made my way to his dressing room he was in the process of asking someone if they had seen me. As soon as he turned around and realized I was in the room, he walked over and gave me a sweet, sweaty kiss. He was soaking wet. I had never seen a singer up-close after a performance, so I didn't realize how much energy they used on the stage.

"Thank you for coming, babe. When did you get here, to Atlanta, I mean?" His smile spread across the length of his face.

"I've been here since 3:00 this afternoon."

The smile disappeared from his face. "Why didn't you call me or come by my room?"

"I didn't think I needed to see you before you performed."

"No, please, for real, don't ever do that again. I was worried, wondering where you were. Next time find me right after you check in and get yourself situated. Well, at least call me and let me know you made it."

I gently grabbed his chin and kissed him again. "I promise, I'll do it just like that from now on."

We rode back to the hotel together in a black Escalade with blacked-out windows. One bodyguard road in the SUV with us and two others rode in another SUV behind us. Groupies and fans were already all over the place when we pulled up to the St. Regis Hotel, so we were taken around to the back entrance to enter the hotel through a secure, underground garage.

As we were getting out of the car, Julian looked over at me. "Baby, you are coming to the after party, right?"

"No, that was not part of our agreement." I shook my head. "I said I would come to your concerts, but I have no intention of going to any of the after parties. You go on to the party and we can meet tomorrow for breakfast or something."

Julian did a sad face and hugged me. "Not even for a little while?"

"Not even for a little while. I don't even want to know where the party is. You go on and enjoy yourself. I can see you in the morning."

Julian held my hand as we walked into the hotel. "I'm going to take a shower, and then go downtown to the party. I won't be long. I'm just going to make an appearance."

I wasn't concerned because my plan was to go to my room, take a shower, watch a little TV, and then go to sleep.

I don't know what time Julian got back, but the next morning he and I worked out, had breakfast in his suite, and spent the morning talking. For lunch we went to Planet Hollywood, just to get out of the hotel. I also hung out with him later in the afternoon when he went to the civic center to soundcheck his equipment. I decided I would skip his Saturday night performance and wait for him at the hotel. Sunday morning we worked out in the hotel gym, then went to the hotel spa, and later had breakfast. The rest of the day we hung out in the hotel and watched videos. I flew home after Julian's Sunday performance. One concert down and three to go.

After every concert I came back and gave Tracie and Kyomi a blow by blow of where I stayed and what I did while I was there; how the women acted during and after the concert; and anything else newsworthy. While Julian was on the road, Tracie, Kyomi, and I sometimes spent the night at his house. We rented videos and watched them on the movie screen in his entertainment room, and then we got up the next morning and worked out in his weight room. This was my way of making up for not inviting them to the party that Julian had for my family when they visited. I sincerely forgot about them because I was so excited about my family meeting Julian. In Kyomi's words, "How are you going to forget about your friends?" She was right, but I did.

In addition to making up for forgetting about them, I also made them aware that I would be neglecting them when Julian got back in town, so we needed to spend some time together doing what we do best, talking.

"So, have you told Julian that you love him?"

"Please, why would I tell him that?" I sat down and looked at Kyomi, wondering what was next.

"You ought to be ashamed of yourself for acting like that. You know we know, right? You can try and fool yourself, but that's the only person you're fooling."

"Shelby, you talk with him almost every night. You've traveled to four different cities to be with him, just so y'all wouldn't miss each other while he's on the road. You have free reign of his house. Girl, you look at that man like you're just going to eat him up. Both of you are just oblivious to everything and everybody that might have the misfortune of being in a room with you. Now, I'm thinking, somebody loves somebody in this scenario. Everybody knows Julian loves you, so I'm with Kyomi on this one. I believe you're in love with him, too. You know?"

Okay, so yeah, I'm in love with him, but I wasn't going to tell them that. Julian and I still hadn't been together long enough for me to expose myself to him like that yet. I have to know for myself that I could love him unconditionally, like I want to. We still have a little way to go.

I could have bet big bucks that Smokie was going to call me as soon as he got back in town. For whatever reason, he made it back before Julian and my phone rang right at 7 o'clock Monday evening.

"Hello, Black Beauty. I told Julian I would call and check on you as soon as I got back. Are you doing all right?"

"Smokie, I thought I told you it wasn't necessary for you to call me for Julian, even if he asked you to." I started laughing because I knew there was nothing I could say that would mean a thing to him. I don't even know if he was listening to me.

"Look here, Shelby, I'm still mad at you for not introducing me to your sister when she was in town. I heard she was fine. I knew there had to be some more like you at home. Since you can't get with me, the least you could do is introduce a brother to your people."

Smokie was a good-looking man, but I wouldn't fix him up with friend or foe.

"Smokie, you already have more women than any man should have. You know I'm not going to set you up to my sister."

He laughed from his gut. "A brother don't need for you to do anything but introduce him. Once she meets me, it won't take long for us to do a little 'sumthin, sumthin.' You know what I'm sayin'?"

I knew we couldn't have a decent conversation. I was going to hang up before I got mad. "Uh, uh, Smokie, you're nasty. Do you really think you're all that, and that every woman you meet wants to go to bed with you? If you do then something is wrong with you and I don't even want to hear about it. Good night, Smokie."

"Next time your people are in town, I can show you better than I can tell you. I got it going on like that." He seemed to laugh more to himself this time. "You have a good night too, Shelby. I'm just getting back to town and my little freaks didn't come to see me while I was on the road, so I got some business to take care of."

And then the phone went silent.

I was so pissed I didn't know what to do. He talked about what he wanted to do to my sister, and then he hung up after calling me a freak.

By the time Julian arrived I had forgotten all about Smokie. Julian wanted to call me as soon as his plane landed at 8:46 p.m., but apparently a large crowd of his fans were at the airport to welcome him back. It was nice watching his career blow up so beautifully.

"Look, I'm calling you from the car. I can ask Mr. Vestas to swing by and pick you up."

"Julian...that would mean I have to spend the night, and you know that's out of the question."

"You spent the night when your family was here and nothing happened."

I knew what would happen if I spent the night this time, though. I had talked with Julian three or four times during the last week and it had only been two weeks since the last time I saw him, but I missed him like I hadn't seen him for the entire three months he was on the road.

I took a deep sigh. "Okay, what if I meet you at your house?"

"It really wouldn't be a problem to come by and get you."

"No, I'll meet you there."

"I wish you'd let us come by and pick you up, but, okay, I'll see you in a little while."

When I arrived, he hugged me like we were reuniting after not seeing each other for years. It felt good to be in his arms. I melted as he held me. For real, I wanted to stand right there for the rest of the night, but, unfortunately, real life ain't even like that. We spent the night talking about how well his first concert tour had gone; how much we missed each other; how groupies act; and the things that his crew did while they were on the road. Before I knew it, it was 1 o'clock in the morning and I needed to get home. The next day was a workday for me. Fortunately, Julian didn't pressure me t to stay.

"I'm going to come by your house to pick you up at 7:00 tomorrow evening, so leave your schedule open."

"What do have planned?"

"It's a surprise." He pulled me close and hugged me. "It's a surprise. Let me surprise you, girl."

I let it go and mentally prepared myself for another surprise. It took some adjusting to…to being treated so good.

He walked me out to my car and kissed me good night before I sped off.

The next day couldn't go by fast enough. I didn't talk with Julian all day, but I talked with Kyomi and Tracie for about 30 minutes after I got home from work. I called Tracie, and then made a three-way call to Kyomi. We talked about what we thought my surprise might be.

Tracie and Kyomi seemed to think Julian was going to ask me to marry him, but I really didn't think he was going to do that. I hadn't even told the man that I loved him yet. When my doorbell rang I was almost ready to go, so I hung up the phone and rushed to the door. As soon as I opened it, I gave Julian a kiss and told him to have a seat while I put my lipstick on. Instead, he followed me into the bathroom to watch me. He stood behind me and wrapped his arms around my waist and kissed me on the back of my neck.

"Mr. Brishard, how do you expect me to do this with you kissing all over me?"

He stopped and looked at our reflection in the mirror. "I don't care if you don't put any lipstick on, you're beautiful without it." Then he kissed me on the back of my neck again. "Don't we look good together?"

I turned my head slightly to the right, cupped his chin, and gave him a peck on the lips. "Yes, sir, we are kind of cute together, huh?"

I finished getting ready and we finally made it out to his car.

"Okay, so tell me, where are we going?"

"You like poetry, right?"

"Of course, I do."

"And you like jazz, right?

"Yeah, why?"

He never answered me, so that made me even more curious to know where he was taking me. First, we went to dinner. While we were eating I kept catching Julian looking at me.

"What are you staring at? Do I have some food on my face or something?" I dabbed at both sides of my mouth with my napkin.

He shook his head. "I like looking at you. You're beautiful."

"Oh, okay, thank you." I blushed.

After dinner we headed for Songs of Solomon, a popular little coffee house on a trendy part of downtown. When we arrived, Julian had the car valet parked and, hand in hand, we walked in. Julian found us a table front and center. The lights were very dim, so most of the people that saw us come in didn't seem to recognize him. We ordered herbal tea and listened to the poem that was being read. I'm always amazed by the amount of untapped talent in these places. All of the spoken word performed moved me. It wasn't long before a very handsome guy with locs was introduced. The name of his poem was, *I've Known Your Love All Along*. As he began to read, he made eye contact with me and slightly bowed his head:

*I felt the heat from your gaze across the room*

*When I turned to see your face your smile embraced my soul*

*When you said hello, I heard a melody that sounded just like love, and the movement of your lips was fluid and smooth*

*Memories of our love ran through my mind—warm breezes, setting suns, love, tears, sleepless nights, smiles, kisses, passion…hot*

*And all of this…before I even knew your name*

*Baby, that's what I call you now, you have me sprung
on the honey of your kisses and the rhythm in your hips
    And that same fluid and smooth movement of your
    lips...when you call out my name
    So now I hold you in my arms and every night I hold
you even closer in my dreams
    I've felt the warmth of your body and I know
intimately the curve of your spine
    I've known all along your heat, your honey, your
rhythm, your rhyme, and your sweet, sweet melody that
definitely gets sweeter...each time you make me feel your
love is all mine
    Girl, it ain't no secret that I love you and I want you
in my life forever, everybody knows that
    It's the memories of our love that I've known all
along that I want to share with you
    It's the memory of hearing you say "I love you"
because I've known it all along
    I've known your love all along*

A piano and a tenor sax accompanied the artist. The
music was almost as beautiful as the poem. While the
poem was being read Julian gently grasped my right
hand and kissed it. I was thinking, *This guy's lady friend
must be very special*. I looked around the room to see if I
could find her sitting alone at a table. When I turned
back around the poet was standing in front of our table.
He handed me a beautifully wrapped square package and
a dozen peach roses.

"For you, queen."

I looked at Julian then I looked back at the guy standing there. Teary-eyed, I looked back at Julian.

Julian smiled. "It's for you, baby. I love you. It wasn't enough for me to tell you. I wanted everybody else to know, too."

I took the package and the flowers and gently kissed Julian on his lips. Everybody in the room clapped. When I opened the box I found the poem, that had just been read, written on parchment and framed.

I leaned in close to Julian. "Is it okay if we leave?"

There was really no point in staying after receiving my gift.

"If that's what you want, of course."

As we stood up to leave I heard a woman whisper, "I think that's Jules Brishard."

Heads turned and fingers pointed as we walked toward the exit. As we made our way outside I knew what I had to do. I had to stop playing and tell this man I love him. While we waited for the car to be brought around, I placed my flowers on top of my gift and placed both on a nearby bench.

I grabbed Julian by the lapel of his jacket. "Come here. Thank you for the poem and the flowers. I don't know what you're trying to do, but I think it's working. You really know how to make a girl feel special. Every time we're together it just seems to get better and better."

When I kissed him, this time it was different because in my heart I was saying, *Julian, I love you*. Even though I still didn't manage to say the words out loud.

# Chapter 10

I was really surprised when I arrived at work one day and listened to my voicemail messages. I had a message from my ex-husband, Lorenz. I hadn't really talked to him since the divorce hearing. As I listened, it occurred to me he sounded like he had been drinking. The call was so random that I knew for sure it had to be because he had been drinking—the message was left at 1:30 in the morning. It made me kind of sick to my stomach to think he would get drunk then call me. I didn't know if the call meant he was asking for help, missing me, mad at me, or if he was just horny. Who knows and who cares? I wasn't going to worry about it. I didn't need more drama in my life. My hands were full with Julian.

Aside from the crazy voicemail message, my day went by without incident. There were no more calls from Lorenz. He probably spent the whole day feeling bad about calling, if he even remembered making the call. I was glad he didn't call back to apologize. I didn't feel like hearing it. I wanted to have a clear head when I saw Julian later. I didn't know what his calendar looked like, but I was going to invite him to ride home with me for a four day weekend to meet my parents. It was no big deal, though. Well, I guess it really is, but if he can't go I'm sure Tracie and Kyomi would be more than willing to make themselves available to take the ride.

As soon as I was finished at work I called Julian. We had decided the night before that we would meet for an early dinner. Actually, it would be dinner at a normal time for a change. Julian wasn't home when I called and he didn't get home until an hour after I arrived. So, while I waited Miss Gladys and I sat and talked. She was one of the sweetest women I had ever met. I thought it was really nice that she felt comfortable enough to talk to me about Julian. Comfortable isn't quite the correct word, though. She felt like it was her responsibility to tell me how to treat Julian.

"Look here, honey. Julian is like a grandson to me. And I'm only telling you this because he cares so much about you, and you seem like such a nice girl."

"Yes, ma'am."

"The worst thing you can do to him is try to take advantage of his kindness. You understand what I'm saying?"

"Yes, ma'am. I would never do anything to hurt Julian."

I could see how that would be easy to do because he didn't believe in holding back. If he felt like doing something, he did it, and if he felt like saying something, he said it. You always knew where he was coming from.

"If you hurt him, Shelby, I'll make it my business to keep you away from him."

That was the last thing Miss Gladys said to me before Julian arrived. It sounded like that nice, little, old lady was threatening me. I have to admit, it was kind of cute.

Julian finally arrived and Miss Gladys left for the night. He and I sat down and had dinner, which was as good a time as any to talk about the trip.

"Sooo, do you think you want to go meet my parents this weekend?"

"Baby, no…"

"No?"

"No, not like that. I mean, no, I can't go this weekend. Ah, man, I have to go out of town Friday morning. I'll be gone for a week."

I was a little disappointed, but only because I had kind of worked myself up about the trip. I knew his schedule was peculiar.

"You have my word, I'll make time real soon to meet your folks."

"I know you will."

Before we finished dinner the phone rang. Julian excused himself.

"Babe, I have to take this call."

He talked on the phone for a few minutes then handed it to me.

"Here, it's for you."

"What? Who would be calling me over here?"

"Here, just take the phone." Julian smiled at me mischievously.

I reached up and took the phone from his hand. "Hello?"

"Hi, how are you, Shelby?"

"I'm sorry, I have no idea…"

"I am so sorry, Julian should have told you. I'm Hallie Rose, his mother."

"Oh, I'm so sorry." I hit Julian with my free hand. "It's nice to meet you, Ms. Rose."

"He should have done this a little differently, but I've heard a lot about you. My mother and I are looking forward to meeting you some time soon."

"Ms. Rose, I'm looking forward to meeting you and your mother, as well. It's really nice to get a chance to talk with you." I mean mugged Julian as I spoke with his mother.

"I certainly didn't mean to put you on the spot, but he told me to hold on, so I think he got both of us." She laughed at her son's misplaced sense of humor.

"Please tell your mother I said hello."

"Oh, I certainly will. She'll be glad to hear that we spoke. We were beginning to think he made you up, to stop us from talking about him settling down." I could feel her smile through the phone.

I looked over at Julian and put my hand over the mouthpiece of the phone. "Do you need to speak to your mother again?"

Pleased, he smiled and shook his head from side-to-side.

"Ms. Rose, again, it was really a pleasure to finally meet you. I think Julian and I are going to finish dinner, so I can, uhm, go home soon."

"He didn't tell me y'all were having dinner. You two, go ahead, finish dinner and I'm sure we'll talk again soon. Please tell Julian I'll talk with him tomorrow."

"I will, good night."

After I ended the call, I crossed my arms over my chest. "I can't believe you did that. How are you just going to hand me the phone like that?"

"What? I knew y'all would get along fine."

"That's not the point, Julian Brishard. Oh, my gosh, I cannot believe you. Don't ever do that again. Do you know how uncomfortable that was?"

"Baby, that was just my mom. She's cool and everything. She would never say anything out of the way." He reached across the table, as if I might uncross my arms and reach out to touch his hand.

"You know what? I can't even finish eating. We might as well clear the table off."

"Finish eating? You don't have much left on your plate to eat anyway." He chuckled to himself, and then playfully made a sad face.

I stood up, grabbed my plate, and headed for the kitchen.

"Wait, baby, no, don't be like that. Don't walk out." Laughing, he got up and followed behind me.

It was 8:00 p.m., so after cleaning our plates off and putting them in the dishwasher, we went into the entertainment room to watch a movie. We plopped down on the couch and I curled up with my back up against his chest. Lying there felt good and made up for making me talk with his mom. When he threw his arm around me and rested his hand on my belly it felt even better. It wasn't long before Julian was whispering in my ear.

"Shelby, tell me why you make me so happy? What do you do to me, girl?

I laughed. "You're silly. I don't do anything to you."

"Uh, uh...*Tell me where you came from and when you're going to take me there / You know there's nothing I wouldn't do for you...*"

As he sang he placed sweet, little kisses on my ear and the back of my neck. I turned my head so that I could taste the sweetness. Without even thinking about it, I sat up and laid back. Before I knew it, Julian was on top of me. I liked the weight of his body on top of mine. Whether he knew it or not, he was in control. I felt his hand running up and down the outside of my thigh. When he found the small of my back I think I moaned a little. I snapped back to reality when he began to whisper in my ear again.

"Stay with me tonight, Shell."

Okay, I didn't know how I was going to get out of this situation. There was no one to burst through the door this time. Julian was on top of me, his hands were all over me, and he was asking me to spend the night with him. The easiest thing to do was the most obvious, but also the most abrupt.

"Julian, we better stop."

I tried to push him off of me, but I don't know if I wasn't strong enough or if I was just going through the motion. I had to make Julian stop before things went too far.

This time I said it a little louder and with a little more force. "Julian, please, stop."

"Baby, nothing will change if you don't leave tonight. Stay with me."

I found myself pushing him a littler harder than I think he even expected. "Get...off of me...Julian! I'm not staying."

He stopped, looked at me, and slowly stood up. "I'm sorry." He sighed, his hand over his mouth and chin.

Julian walked across the room and stood with his back to me, as he rested the back of his head in his clenched hands.

I sat up and tightly closed my eyes. "Maybe I should leave."

Julian didn't make a sound. Instead, he threw his head back in his hands.

When I finally stood up, I slid my shoes on, but I couldn't remember where my purse was. My head was in a fog as I walked around looking for it. I wanted to hurry and leave, just so the moment would be over. There had to be a way to let Julian know it wouldn't always be like this, and that I knew how hard it was for him because it was hard for me too. After I found my purse on the kitchen counter I went back to let Julian know I was leaving. When I found him, he was sitting on the couch looking at TV.

I reluctantly walked back into the room. "I'm going to leave now." I spoke softly and tentatively.

He slowly got up to walk me to the door.

An uncomfortable silence accompanied us as we made our way to the front door. I wondered what he was thinking. When I opened the door we both stood there for a few seconds and peered out at my car. I gathered my thoughts and turned around to face him.

"Can I get a good night hug?" I reached for him.

The firmness of his hug—the firmness that I had grown accustom to—was still there. I closed my eyes and placed my head against his chest.

"I'm sorry, Julian."

Julian cradled my head with his hand. "Yeah, I know, me too."

When I looked up at him, he gently held my face and kissed me on my forehead.

"Good night, baby."

"I'll call you." I gave him a half smile as I slowly backed out of his arms.

He nodded.

I started my car and drove out of the driveway. I glanced back at Julian as he stood in the doorway and watched me drive away. A short distance down the street, I pulled over and rested my forehead on the steering wheel. Maybe I was asking him for too much. He could hold me, kiss me, hug me, and even love me, but no matter how turned on he got I wasn't going to let him make love to me. Was I being unreasonable? Maybe I should break things off. Did I really have to be that dramatic? I pulled the rearview mirror down and looked at myself: *You're so silly, sitting on the side of the road making what could be a life altering decision. You just need to make up your mind, but first you need to get off of the side of the road and go home.*

When I got home I immediately checked my answering machine ... no Julian. I took a quick shower and dressed for bed. As I walked toward my bed I looked at the phone and wondered if I should call him. By the time I crawled under the covers I decided we needed to talk while things were still fresh on our minds. I could feel my heart beating in my chest as Julian's phone rang several times. All kinds of thoughts ran through my head: *Maybe he called someone over to relieve the tension; maybe he had gone over to another woman's house...* When he finally answered he sounded like he had been sleeping—that never crossed my mind.

"I'm sorry, Julian, did I wake you up?"

"It's okay. I'm glad you called."

It made me feel a little better knowing he was still speaking to me.

I took a deep breath and started talking. "I'm sorry about what happened tonight. I let things go too far, again, and I shouldn't have done that. I really feel like we need to talk about it."

There was silence.

"You're right, we do need to talk about it. First of all, though, I want to apologize to you because I lost it for a few minutes. Like I said before, nothing would have changed if you had stayed tonight, but, of course, nothing's going to change because you didn't stay either. I know you want to wait until we're married to make love. Baby, I can't do anything but respect that. I wish I could promise you that I won't get mad or frustrated about it. I guess you just have to teach me how to be patient. This is brand new to me. I've never had to wait before. I've never wanted to either, but I know you're worth waiting for."

Julian had surprised me again. Even though I know what kind of man he is, I thought for sure he was going to say let's not see each other for a while. I wasn't expecting an apology from him. Yet, something was wrong because I was still a little sad.

"Baby, I know this is really difficult for you because it's also difficult for me. I've been thinking about this ever since I left your house. I feel like I'm asking you for too much." I paused for just a second to gather my thoughts. "If you want to see other people, Julian, I'll understand. Our relationship would have to change, of course, but having you in my life has meant so much that I'm willing to hold on to our friendship any way that I can. I want you to be happy…I want to make you happy. I know our relationship isn't about sex, but if that's something that's really important to you …"

Julian laughed. "Shelby, stop, okay. I'd like to believe that I'm a little deeper than that. You mean a lot more to me than just sex, but I ain't going to lie to you. I'd be less than a man if I sat here and said I didn't want to have sex with you. Look, over the last few years I've met a lot of women who've wanted to be a part of my life because of who I am and the things that I've acquired. Most of them didn't really want 'me,' and to be honest with you, I didn't really want to be with them either. They were good for the moment.

The very first day I saw you I knew I was going to love you. When you smiled at me I knew you were going to love me back. I could tell that you were going to bring something to my life that was missing. I guess, what I'm saying is, if I have to wait another lifetime to make love to you, then, I guess, I'll just have to wait. This might sound like a line, but I find waiting kind of sexy. Frustrating, but sexy." He laughed loud, like he couldn't even believe what he was saying. "Girl, we'll be all right. If this is the biggest problem we ever have then we don't have any problems, right? I know I got you." He chuckled. "I know you belong to me, so…"

Was there anything the man could say to make me love him less? "Since you put it like that, I guess you're right." I smiled. "You know I belong to you, huh?"

"Psss…girl, yeah."

The way he spoke to me turned me on a little bit. I belong to him. He didn't say it like I was his property, more like I was something 'special' that belonged just to him.

"I guess I should start worrying when I find something to worry about, huh?"

"Yep."

Everything seemed to be okay.

Julian interrupted my thoughts. "If we're all straight now, I think I'm going to go to bed because 'not' making love to you has worn me out."

I laughed. "You're so silly. Okay, then, I guess it's good night."

"Yep, good night. Oh, can I get a good night kiss?"

Nothing had changed and everything was going to be all right after all.

# Chapter 11

A couple of days went by before I went over to Julian's again. I had to work on my self-control. Smokie showed up with a girl, well, a very attractive woman, whose skirt was so short that if she had bent over I would have gotten to know her personally, and if she had sneezed, or even taken a really deep breath, her breasts would have popped out of her tiny blouse. She was Julian's ex, so it didn't take a rocket scientist to figure out she was going to be trouble. As they walked into the entertainment room, Smokie announced their entrance.

"Hey, Shelby, baby. Ju'man, look who I found wandering around outside, Camilla the man killa." He laughed hard at what appeared to be a private joke.

"Hello…"

The chick spoke, but never even looked at me. She immediately turned her attention to Julian, who was sitting right next to me.

"Julian, I need to talk to you…now."

I turned and looked at him as if to say, *I know she's not coming in here ordering people around and I know you're getting ready to show her the door*.

Julian stood up. "Shell, I'll be right back." Then he walked out of the room with 'Camilla, the man killa.'

Smokie was loving every minute of whatever had just happened. "You trust her with your man, huh? She ain't no joke and talk about a freak. They don't come no freakier. It ain't no secret that I've had a piece of that. Look here, you need to get with the program. Go ahead and hook my brother Ju'man up. I know you capable 'cause you built like a prize winning quarter horse. Then you need to come on over and let Smokie love you down. I promise you won't be disappointed. Look at Camilla, she can't stay away from here." He laughed so hard I thought he was going to hyperventilate.

I didn't see the humor. I sat there and looked at him because I couldn't believe how he was tripping. The more I thought about it the madder I got. So, instead of saying anything to him, I got up to go see what was taking Julian so long. Smokie stood up too. He swaggered over to the bar and fixed himself a drink.

He looked over at me as he poured some vodka over ice. "You need a drink, sweetheart? You might need to hurry up and take care of your business, for real." He started laughing as he lifted his drink up to his lips.

The more he laughed the madder I got. "Smokie, something is wrong with you. You aren't right, but you know that, don't you? Sometimes you just make me sick; you really make me sick."

I knew he wasn't paying any attention to what I was saying, so I left the room to look for my man. I didn't know what to expect when I found Julian and Camilla, but I knew Julian wouldn't disappoint me...I hoped. I went to the kitchen and they weren't there. Actually, I didn't think they would be, but my nerves made me go to the least obvious place first. I then went through the dining room to get to the living room. I finally heard them in the foyer.

"Look, Camilla you need to leave. I'll talk with you later."

"I want to know why you can't talk with me now."

She was crying.

I couldn't believe she was in his house tripping while I was there. I thought, *I'm going to have to bust this up because girlfriend is going to give me my respect. Julian is being way too nice for me*. Just as I was about to walk into the foyer Julian started talking again.

"Come on, now, Camilla. It hasn't been like that in a long time. That doesn't work anymore."

She was still crying. "But, baby, you know I need you. Let's just go up to your room. You know how good I used to make you feel. Nothing has changed. I can make you forget about Sheila, or whatever her name is. I can make you feel better than she does."

*Did she just call me Sheila?* Okay, it was time for me to intervene. Enough was enough, so I walked into the foyer.

"Julian, what's going on? Is everything all right out here?"

Camilla's arms were up around Julian's neck and Julian was wrestling to get them off of him. When they realized I was there everything stopped. Camilla's arms dropped down to her side and she turned her head so that I couldn't see that she was crying. I walked over to Julian and put my arm around his waist and looked at Camilla.

"I'm sorry, is there something I can help you with Camilla? You look upset."

"You can't do a thing for me." She glared at me as she spoke. "Julian, I'll talk with you later."

With that said, she stormed out the door and quickly jumped in her car and sped off. She never looked back.

I was so pissed I didn't know what to do. The first thing I did, though, was to take my arm from around Julian then I turned and looked at him.

"What was up with her? I mean, what was that all about?"

Julian looked kind of agitated. "Look, baby, I really don't want to talk about it right now." He started walking away.

I thought, *I don't care how you feel, you need to tell me something*.

I grabbed his arm. "Uhm, excuse me, Julian, but some half-naked woman comes into your house while I'm here and tries to talk you into going to bed with her; I don't know what you say about that, but she disrespected me. Then you tell me that you don't want to talk about it right now? Uh, uh…no."

Julian turned and looked at me. "Look, I don't need you trippin', too. You either trust me or you don't. Either way, I'm not going to talk about it right now." As he turned to walk away I heard him say something under his breath. "Women are a trip."

Well, since he wasn't going to talk about it and he was headed back to the entertainment room, I guess that was supposed to be the end of it, but it was far from over. I didn't want to continue this in front of Smokie because I knew he would only make matters worse. When I walked into the entertainment room Smokie was ready to start some more trouble.

"Where's Camilla? Did you give her the boot, Shelby?"

I acted like I didn't hear him.

"Man, don't let her in my house anymore. She's even crazier than she was when we were kickin' it." Julian fixed himself a drink, and then looked at me. "You want one?"

I shook my head and sat down across the room. I looked at Smokie as I bit my bottom lip. *He knew what he was doing when he let her in.* While I was looking at him he blew me a kiss. I sighed and turned my head. I can't figure him out. I was too aggravated to hang around, so now was as good a time as any to leave. I wanted to talk about Camilla and I wasn't going to do it with Smokie there, so I stood up to leave.

"Julian, you know what? I think I'm going to go home."

Julian grabbed my hand as I walked passed him. "Baby, don't leave, I want you to stay."

I looked at him, and then back at Smokie. Julian knew what I was trying to say.

"Man, don't you have somewhere you're supposed to be?"

Smokie smiled. "Nah, I want to stay here with y'all." Then he stood up. "Yeah, matter of fact, I do have somewhere I can go. If I drive fast enough I might be able to catch up with your girl."

Julian pulled me close to him. "That ain't funny man."

As soon as I thought Smokie was gone I started talking. "Why did Smokie do that?"

Julian looked at me as if he was puzzled. "Do what? What did my boy do?"

I stepped back and looked at him. "Smokie knew I was here and he brought that woman in the house anyway."

Julian looked at me with his brow wrinkled. "How was Smokie supposed to know you were here? Aren't you parked around back? And why would he do anything to disrespect you, Shelby? He knows you're my lady and he knows how I feel about you. I can't believe you're trippin' like this. I know what you're really mad about. Let me assure you, Camilla won't be coming over here anymore. You heard me tell Smokie not to let her in my house again, and tomorrow I'll tell her she's not welcome over here. Problem solved."

Julian had not made me feel any better. As a matter of fact, I had gotten a little more upset. He was acting like this whole situation with Smokie and Camilla was no big deal.

"Wait, wait, wait. First of all, why has she been coming over here anyway? Second of all, what's up with Smokie? He told me he slept with her. Excuse me if I'm a little confused, but if you were dating her, what was he doing having sex with her? Is that something y'all do often, share women? 'Cause if it is, I'm not the one. Plus, I don't like Smokie always trying to pull up on me. If he's your boy, and everything, then you need to tell him to stop. Sometimes he really makes me feel uncomfortable and I'm getting to the point that I don't want him around when I'm with you."

Julian shook his head. "Whoa, baby, I'm not going to choose between you and Smokie, so I hope that's not what you're asking me to do. That's just Smokie talking. I've already told you that he's not going to disrespect you because you are 'my lady.' But just so it's clear, if I'm with a woman and she does get it on with my boy, she can't be my lady anymore. That's the story of Camilla, and as far as who comes to my house is concerned, this is my house, and I think that's all that needs to be said about that. I'm not going to disrespect you and I'm not going to let anyone else disrespect you because I love you, plain and simple."

Both of us stood there for a few seconds. The seconds felt like forever, though.

Finally, I got a chance to say something. "Look, you're upset and I'm upset, so I'm going to leave. I need the fresh air anyway. This whole scene tonight is messing with my head."

As I turned to leave the room, Julian grabbed me. "Baby, you don't need to leave, and anyway I want you to stay."

I shook my head. "Uh, uh, for real...I need to go."

Julian sighed. "Okay...but can I at least get a kiss before you leave me?"

"I shouldn't..." I looked at him and rolled my eyes.

Julian smiled. "But we both know you want to."

We kissed, and then he held my hand as he walked me through the kitchen to my car. When we got to the car I turned and faced him.

"Don't fool me, Julian."

Julian put his hands on either side of my waist. "I can't fool you, Miss Simone. I love you." Then he kissed me again.

I looked over at Julian as I drove down the driveway. As had become his custom, Julian watched me as I pulled away.

# Chapter 12

It took me a few days to finally get over the scene at Julian's house. It was a good thing he was out of town. Tracie knew something was wrong with me, but she's not one to put pressure on anybody. And, anyway, she knew I would eventually tell her and Kyomi what was going on.

"So, this video chick—okay, I'm thinking she's a video chick because I have never seen that much breast and booty in person before—came waltzing up in Julian's house trippin', begging him to have sex with her!"

Tracie laughed. "Deg." Then she stopped and looked at me. "Deg."

Kyomi was ready to get all up in somebody's face. "Who is the tramp? You need to tell her what she really is."

All of this and she had never even met the woman.

Tracie looked at me with her face twisted. "So, what you gonna do? I take it you haven't talked with Julian in a couple of days? What y'all gonna do?"

Kyomi jumped right in. "What is Julian's phone number? I want to talk with him myself. What is his problem? I can't believe he let some woman trip out like that while you were there. Give me the telephone. He is not going to have other women disrespecting you. If she's an ex-girlfriend then she needs to just step off."

I looked up at Kyomi because she had jumped up and was flaying her arms all over the place. "Get over it; I have. I had a couple of days to think about it and I came to the conclusion that Camilla was just an irate, ex-girlfriend that Julian really didn't have anything to do with anymore."

In spite of my grandstanding, maybe it was my insecurities getting the best of me, but Julian and I were still going to have to talk about women coming to his house, particularly when I'm not there. Actually, I don't want them there when I'm there either. Now, Smokie. I still couldn't figure out what his problem was. Sometimes I really liked him and sometimes I couldn't stand him. I made up my mind to talk with Julian, again, about his friend. I didn't know how it was going to turn out because Julian made it clear he wasn't going to choose between the two of us. I knew I had to at least let him know how I felt.

Tracie gave me the best advice. "You know, Julian hasn't called you because he thinks you're still mad with him. Why don't you call him and invite him over when he gets back? Just think, y'all will be on neutral ground, no Smokie, no other women. But then again, girl, you don't need me to tell you what to do. I don't have a man."

We got a laugh out of that, but she was right. I needed to call Julian to let him know that I wasn't upset. While they were still at my house I called him at his hotel. Kyomi and Tracie made faces at me the entire time I was on the phone. They can be such teenagers sometimes. It was good to hear his voice, though. I could tell he was smiling and that made me happy. We made plans to meet at my place after he got back in town on Friday. After I hung up the phone, I must have been grinning from ear to ear.

Tracie pointed at me. "Ooh, he must have said something mighty, mighty good."

I laughed at her. "No, I just thought about something. We're going to have dinner on Friday, and Thursday is our one-year anniversary. It's been a whole year since we first met."

Even though Kyomi liked Julian, she was still a little upset by the incident with Camilla. "I guess you're going to do something special…for the occasion, I mean?"

"No, just dinner, but I think I'll go and get him a gift tomorrow during lunch. What do you think I should get him?"

Kyomi looked at me and rolled her eyes. "I don't know, maybe some kind of restraint."

I didn't get a chance to talk with Julian on Thursday because he had a few radio interviews before he came back to town. When he got back it was late, so he didn't call me, but the first voice I heard when I woke up on Friday morning was his. He called and woke me up for work.

"Good morning, baby girl, are you up yet?"

I smiled and stretched. "Uhhhhh…no, but good morning anyway. What are you doing up so early?"

"I wanted to be the first one to say good morning to you and I wanted to tell you about the date I'm going on this evening. I've been seeing this lady for a minute. She's a tall, beautiful, black, Amazonian princess."

"Is she good to you?"

He laughed. "What? Man, she's the best thing that has happened to me in years."

"If she's so good to you, why isn't she your queen?"

"I've been wondering the same thing, but, you know, she's real serious about her business. She's not my queen because she hasn't given the word that we can get married yet, but after we're married, though, she'll be the queen of my everything."

Knowing him and loving him sometimes felt like make believe. He's exactly the kind of guy that you dream of  meeting, even though you think he really doesn't exist. We agreed to have dinner at 7:00 p.m. and Julian promised he wouldn't be late.


My workday went by without incident. It was actually a pretty dull day. During lunch I met Tracie at the mall and she helped me pick out an anniversary gift for Julian. I needed help because I couldn't imagine what to get the man. He has enough money to get anything he wants. We ended up picking out a very nice silk robe with a pair of matching boxers. On the way home from work I picked up some fresh asparagus, chicken divan, already prepared, a mushroom and mixed green salad, and some raspberry vinaigrette salad dressing, and, of course, I got us a couple of bottles of wine. Even though Julian doesn't eat a lot of sweets, I still bought a small German chocolate cheesecake for desert.

It was hard to believe it had been a whole year since I first met Julian. He and I had grown from meeting each other at a restaurant, to seeing each other on an almost daily basis. To me, the relationship was progressing at a nice pace, not too fast, not too slow. I suppose, things could move a little faster if I would just tell Julian how much I actually love him. Maybe by this time next year I'll be Mrs. Julian Brishard. I liked the way that sounded—Mrs. Julian Brishard.

When Julian arrived he was gorgeous. He had on a black blazer, a dark red, raised print, semi-sheer, button-up shirt, with the two top buttons open, black slacks, and a silver chain. I also loved his black lace up shoes, with the crossover buckle strap. The boy really has good taste in clothes and, to prove it, he looked good from head to toe. When I opened the door he held up two dozen white tulips.

"Happy anniversary."

See, that's what I mean, what other man would remember a one-year anniversary? And not only had he remembered our anniversary, but he also bought my favorite flowers. I gave him a great big ole' kiss, grabbed him by the hand and pulled him in the door. I hurried in the kitchen to get a vase for my flowers. I moved the candles off of the dining room table and put the flowers there instead. Julian made himself comfortable to Mint Condition playing in the living room.

"If I didn't know any better, I would think you were trying to seduce a brother. You're pretty smooth, Shelby Simone, wine chilling, music playing, scented candles burning, gotcha' little black dress on. Yeah, you tryin' to mess a brother's head up. You know I'm right." He bit his lip and playful nodded his head.

I brought Julian a glass of wine and sat down next to him on the couch. "Mr. Brishard, I have no idea what you're talking about, but thank you again for the tulips. I love them."

We talked for about 30 minutes, even though I could have sat there listening to him all night. Eventually, I got up and set the dining room table. During dinner we talked some more, until I started clearing the table off.

"Do you want some dessert?"

"No, babe, looking at you is like having dessert— sweet, dark, chocolate."

I laughed and hit his hand. "That was kind of corny, but you're still a smooth talker."

After dinner we went back into the living room and sat on the couch. I gave him his gift and watched him smile as he opened it. He pulled the robe out of the box and held it up then he pulled the boxers out and held them up, too.

"Thank you, baby." He looked up at me. "How did you know what size I wore?"

As he held the red, black, and dark gold paisley print boxers up in the air, I imagined how good he was going to look in them. He must have been reading my mind.

"I can't wait to show you how good I look in them."

I smiled, but refrained from responding.

"Come over here." Julian pulled me up against his chest. He took his hands and gently placed them on either side of my face and kissed me. "Thank you for another perfect night. Oh, wait a minute." He pulled a little jewelry box from his jacket pocket. "This must be for you."

He handed me the little, black, velvet box and watched as I slowly opened it. It was a pair of two-carat diamond, studs. My heart almost led me to believe it was going to be an engagement ring. The earrings were beautiful, though. I was really surprised and he knew it. I hugged him and kissed him all over his face.

He held me tight. "You know, Shell, I've never felt this way about anybody before. Everything about this, us, has been new to me. Thank you for dinner tonight and thank you for letting me into your life. If you had said no the first time I saw you things would have been very different. You might have been sitting here with some knucklehead or I might have stalked you until I got your phone number." He stopped and smiled. "What do you think we can do next year to top this?"

"I don't know, but it's been a good year for me, too. After I realized my marriage was really over, I had no idea I was making room for you. I know one thing; it feels good to be happy. So, thank you, Mr. Brishard." I gently stroked his cheek. "Can I ask you something, though? Do you think we'll always be this happy?" I had second thoughts as soon as the words slid passed my lips. "Never mind. That was silly, don't answer that. I know we can do this."

"I know we can do it, too, Shell."

Julian got up to leave a little after 2:00 in the morning. "You sure you don't want me to stay and model my robe for you?"

"Boy, let me tell you something. If you put those boxers on, I can assure you Julian Brishard would never want to leave here." I smiled mischievously.

"Oh, so you gonna' tease me? That's not fair. You play too much."

"You're right, I do. I apologize. That was uncalled for…no matter how true it is."

We kissed and said good night. We made plans to meet tomorrow and go to a matinee. It was good to know that after a year the newness of our relationship hadn't worn off.

On Saturday Kari and Sharrin made a three-way call to me to ask if they could come to town and hang out with me in three weeks. Of course I had no problem with that, but I was sure more was involved.

"Kari, what are y'all really coming up here for?"

Kari laughed. "Because you are our baby sister and we love you and miss you and we want to see you."

I knew that wasn't it. "Okay, I'm going to ask one more time. What is the real reason why y'all are coming here? It wouldn't have anything to do with Julian, would it?"

I only asked because Kari usually traveled with her husband and kids. She didn't leave them behind too often.

Finally, Sharrin broke down. "Kari wants to meet Julian. But, I don't understand why we can't be coming there to check on you, though. You act like we don't love you or something."

They both laughed.

I knew they loved me. I figured, if Coco could come to town and hang out with my friend than what's to make me think my sisters wouldn't do the same thing. Coco had actually come to town on two or three occasions with some of his boys and hung out with Julian, clubbing and partying. The only reason I even knew he was in town was because Julian called and told me he was at his house. So, now Kari and Sharrin were coming to visit. I would have to ask Julian if we could stay at his place the weekend they were in town. I'm sure he wouldn't have a problem with it. As a matter of fact, he would probably be excited about entertaining more of my family.

This time I wouldn't forget about my friends. I invited Tracie and Kyomi to hang out with us, to make it a girls' weekend.

"You do realize this is the first time you've asked us to a party at Julian's.

"Yeah, and your point is what?"

There were times when Kyomi pissed me off; I felt like this was going to be one of those times.

"What's your point, Kyomi?"

"Well, let's see. The only reason you're inviting us is because your sisters are coming to town and you feel guilty that Julian is having a party for them. How does that sound so far?"

"It sounds ridiculous. Anyway, we're talking about staying at Julian's home, not some hotel. Give me a break. Y'all visit out there all of the time and you've even spent weekends there. We've even gone out there to workout. So, what's the big deal? I didn't think you were into that whole party thing anyway?"

She was always going to make her point, no matter how pointless it was.

"All I'm saying is, if you had really wanted us to go to any of the parties out there, you would have invited us before now."

If Kyomi only knew. It's torture for me to be at Julian's house, especially all night, whether other people are there or not. I love him and we have some crazy chemistry going on. Hanging out with him like that does nothing but frustrate us.

I finally conceded. "Yeah, you're right, Kyomi. I never thought about it like that. I should have been more sensitive. So are you going or not?"

Tracie had been sitting there listening the whole time. "I don't know what Kyomi is tripping about. I'm already there."

# Chapter 13

Sharrin and Kari showed up late on a Friday afternoon, so I got off from work a little early to pick them up from the airport. We wouldn't have to stop by my house because I already had my clothes packed and in the car. Tracie and Kyomi were going to meet us at Julian's house around 7 o'clock. As soon as their plane landed Kari called me. She had talked Sharrin into meeting me at the curb, so that I didn't have to pay for parking and come in and find them. When I saw Kari she looked good for a 38-year-old with three kids. She could easily pass for 25. The pickup was quick and easy. I popped my trunk, they threw their luggage in, and then they jumped in the car.

"So, Kari, how are my niece and nephews doing?"

"Like they want to. They're fine. They're clothed, fed, and housed by a mommy and a daddy, so they have no choice but to be fine."

"Do they know that?"

"And take advantage of it every chance they get." She smiled at the truth loaded in her own statements.

"And Sharrin, how's your boyfriend? Does he know you're here visiting me?"

"My boyfriend? You know better than that. I don't remember whether or not I even told my friend I was going out of town. You know me, girl."

"Your friend? Does he know he's just your friend?"

"Well, first, who are you talking about?"

"Girl, you're a trip."

Laughter filled the car because Kari and I were very familiar with how uninhibited Sharrin's dating habits were. She didn't really ever date anyone. She only went out with them, on occasion. I didn't even want to know what she might be doing to keep them around. They never seemed to leave or get mad with her. Whatever it was, I guess she was doing it right.

When we arrived at Julian's house I turned on my right turn signal.

"Is this where your Jules Brishard lives? This is impressive." Kari quickly qualified what she was saying. "It's impressive that such a young man is doing so well for himself."

I understood exactly where she was coming from because one thing that I always admired about my oldest sister was that she was not a materialistic person, nor the least bit pretentious…never was. When we were living at home and guys came by the house to take her out, our mom and dad didn't have to check them out because by the time Kari finished with them, if they came to see her to impress her with their car, jewelry, or clothes, she would have the poor guy nearly in tears as he left. She is definitely a no nonsense kind of gal. I love that about her. I've also learned a lot from her throughout the years. I really have a great deal of respect for her, too, and not just because she's my big sister.

Sharrin, on the other hand, is the party sister. She and Coco are most alike, even though she and Collin are twins. She's always looking for a party. It would stand to reason that she would be the one dating Julian, instead of me. She loves rubbing elbows with the hoity-toity. When we were growing up, she, in fact, was the one that was impressed by the clothes, jewelry, and cars, but her goal was to have her own and not be swayed by someone else's playthings. That is what I love most about Sharrin—she works hard to have the things she likes and to do the things she wants to do. I know, without a shadow of a doubt, that I can always count on having fun when I'm with her. She wouldn't stand for it to be any other way.

I opened the gate and parked my car in the back, so that we could enter the house through the kitchen. Miss Gladys was still there finishing dinner for us, so I introduced her to Kari and reintroduced her to Sharrin. She showed me where the rest of the food was, that she had prepared for us for the weekend. She had taken the time to prepare meals for us for the entire weekend. She put everything in the deep freezer for us to thaw out when we got ready for it. She really takes good care of Julian. Well, to tell the truth, she downright spoils him.

"Well, young ladies, it's time for me to go home, but I tell you the truth, you...are...some...pretty...girls. Now, look here, I know I'm not your mama, but y'all have fun this weekend. Be careful, though. Watch yourselves. Julian is a good boy, but young ladies, like yourself, have to watch out for men, sex, drugs, and liquor.

"Yes, ma'am, I'll keep an eye on these two."

"And who's gone keep and eye on you? You can't be much older than them."

"Oh, yes, ma'am. I'm 38 years old. I'm also married with three children."

Miss Gladys put her hand on her hip and leaned back and looked at Kari. "Well, do tell, do tell. You still young, though." She laughed to herself as she headed for the back door. "Some of Julian's friends are a little rowdy, so I still want y'all to watch out for yourselves."

At that point I interjected. "Like Smokie..."

Miss Gladys stopped and turned around. "Oh, no, he's a nice young man. Always so helpful when he's here."

I grinned at her. "Smokie, really?"

Miss Gladys nodded her head. "I assure you, Smokie is one of the nicest young men that I know, right behind Julian."

"Uh..." I was left speechless.

After Miss Gladys finally left, I escorted Kari and Sharrin upstairs. I chose the bedroom farthest from Julian's room. I was still trying to fool myself into believing the distance between the bedrooms was going to somehow make a difference. Even though it had been two years since the last time I was with a man, I'm a big girl. I'm sure I can handle myself, this time. In the mean time, Sharrin was ready to get the party started. I could hear her down the hall.

"Shelby, what time is Julian getting here and what time is the party starting?"

I screamed back down the hall. "Sharrin, chill out. You have all night to party. Julian should be home in a couple of hours. Relax."

After unpacking we went back downstairs to the kitchen. We decided to postpone eating dinner until Kyomi and Tracie showed up. Instead of eating, I took Kari on a tour of the house. We went to my favorite room, the entertainment room, and my second favorite place at the house, the patio.

"Does he live here alone?"

I looked at Kari. "Yeah, why?"

"Shelby, this is a big house for a single man and, from all of the videos that I've seen him in, he's pretty good looking. So, I'm asking if you're sure no other woman stays here?" When she finished speaking she looked at me with a partial grin on her face.

Even though I didn't appreciate the insinuation, I understood why she was asking, she's just practical like that. "I assure you, Julian is not seeing anyone else, but from time to time his friends, men friends, stay over with their dates, but we're working on changing that. And, anyway, we've been together long enough for me to know no other woman lives here."

She nodded her head and puckered her lips. "Oh, okay."

*What now*?, I thought.

Kari grabbed my hand. "How serious are you about Julian and how serious is he about you? I'm just asking because I don't want you to get hurt. I love you and I know you can handle yourself, but I want to make sure you're not blinded by the lifestyle."

I looked at Kari and smiled. I had forgotten, there was one thing that I not only admired about her, but disliked, as well. She didn't beat around the bush. She always had your best interest at heart … to a fault. It bordered on being obnoxious.

"Kari, when I met Julian I had no idea who he was for about a week and by the end of the first month I liked him anyway. Believe me, I've done a lot of thinking about this relationship. He respects me and he treats me very well. We've been together for a year and he understands that I'm going to be celibate until I'm married. So, it's not like he's taking advantage of me. And, yes, I do think I'm in love with him. He is unbelievably good to me…and for me. We're good for each other. When you meet him you'll see what I'm talking about. You'll like him, watch and see."

"If you love him then I know he can't be too bad. Just be careful." Kari got up, walked over and gave me a hug.

We made our way back to the kitchen and found that Sharrin had fixed herself a plate.

"I was hungry. I couldn't wait another minute."

Kyomi and Tracie came in the back door, so I took them upstairs to unload their luggage, and then we came back downstairs to have some dinner. Well, all of us except Kyomi.

"I told her we were going to have dinner together at Julian's, but she couldn't wait. She stopped on the way and picked up something to eat. You know how she can be sometimes. If she wasn't my friend I really don't think I would be bothered with her one minute." Tracie rolled her eyes and shook her head.

During dinner, Julian arrived. "Well, this is what I like to come home to, a house full of beautiful women."

I got up, walked over to him, and gave him a kiss. "Julian, let me introduce you to my other sister. This is Kari. Kari, Julian."

Kari stood up and shook his hand, right before Julian surprised her with a hug. "It's nice meeting you, Kari. Shelby has told me some really nice things about you. Please make yourself at home while you're here." He stopped and looked at everybody else. "Actually, that goes for all of you, make yourselves at home. You are not considered guests here."

Sharrin looked over at Julian. "So, brother-in-law, what time does the party start?"

He looked at his watch and back up at Sharrin. "You know how it is; the party won't be starting until about 11:00 o'clock, so relax, have some drinks, whatever, until then."

I walked upstairs with Julian. "So, who's coming tonight?"

"You always ask me that and the answer is always the same. It'll be the regulars and Smokie, and then whoever else hears that there's a party."

I had forgotten all about Smokie. I guess, tonight, everybody would get a chance to meet the infamous Smokie.

After I showered and finished getting dressed, I went into everybody else's rooms to see what they were wearing. Kari had on a pair of black hip huggers and a sheer black blouse with a lacy black camisole underneath. Sharrin, on the other hand, was wearing a little red, spaghetti strapped dress, some super sheer red stockings, and a pair of 4 inch red pumps. If it had been anyone else in all of that red, they would have looked like Little Red Riding Hood, but not Sharrin. She was making sure she would be seen and properly talked about during the party. Kyomi, like Kari, was wearing pants and Tracie was struggling over a cute lime green, lace dress or a shiny silver dress. I voted on the lime green dress. I had on a long, brown, straight, spaghetti strapped dress, with a thin, white stripe down both sides and some nice brown, strappy sandals. I was sufficiently cute.

As I was exiting the bedroom that Tracie and I were sharing, I could hear Smokie, making a loud entrance, as he made his way to the living room through the kitchen.

"Okay, let's get this party started. Who's here? Shelby, come on downstairs and dance with me."

He looked upstairs and saw me and Kari standing at the top of the staircase. Sharrin also came out of her room to see what all the fuss was about.

"Who is that screaming like a crazy person?" Kari looked at me then down at Smokie.

I looked at Smokie, who was standing at the bottom of the staircase looking up at us, and then I looked back at Kari. "Kari, I'd like to introduce you to the crazy person, Smokie. Smokie this is my sister, Kari." Sharrin came and stood next to Kari. "Oh, and my other sister, Sharrin."

Smokie uttered an expletive and ran up the stairs, two at a time. "Y'all must come from a family that doesn't have any ugly people in it? Look at y'all. I feel like a kid in a candy store."

Kari put her hand up. "Let me stop you here. I'm married, Shelby is dating Julian, and Sharrin's boyfriend is back home." She quickly looked over at Sharrin after she said that. "So you're actually more like a kid in a china shop. Keep your hands in your pockets and don't touch anything."

Smokie looked down at his feet and started laughing. "I can tell you and Shelby are sisters. Y'all both have that quick wit that I love so much." Then he turned his attention to Sharrin. "Look here, Sharrin? Save the first and the last dance for me 'cause you working that red dress, girl." Smokie walked passed us and went into Julian's room.

Kari looked back at me and pointed at Smokie with her thumb. "That can't be the nice young man Miss Gladys was referring to."

I nodded my head. "Uh, huh, that's him." I continued down the stairs to the kitchen.

I checked the cooler and put a few of the trays in the oven to warm up. Miss Gladys had made about 80 trays of hors'douvres. I don't know how she did it. All I had to do was let the servers in when they arrived. They were very familiar with where everything was. The bartenders didn't need any help either because there were two fully stocked bars that were also stocked with nonalcoholic drinks and bottled water. And when that ran low they knew they could get more liquor from the pantry. While I was walking around checking on everything, Julian walked up behind me and put his arms around me. I love it when he does that. When he kissed me on the side of my neck it sent chills through my body.

"Shell, I'm glad you're here, and look at you. You look good, girl. I want y'all to have a  good time this weekend. Just let me know if I can do anything for you and the rest of the ladies."

I turned around and looked at him, "You're so sweet. Have I told you lately that you spoil me, boy?"

As we kissed, Smokie walked in. "What are y'all doing? Oh, I know. Every time I turn around y'all got your lips all over each other. Y'all better watch out. You gone be in love in a minute." He held his fist up to his lips like he was telling a secret.

I didn't even have a smart remark for him this time because I was in love with Julian and I didn't want to dispute it. Julian and Smokie left the room and went to the entertainment room to turn on the music. As they were walking away I could hear Smokie talking about Sharrin. I wasn't worried about her, though. If anybody could handle him it would be Sharrin.

# Chapter 14

The party was in full swing by 2:30 in the morning. I looked around and Kari was talking with D'Angelo and both Kyomi and Tracie were busy dancing. I hadn't seen Sharrin in a while, so I took a little walk to look for her. The more I thought about it, the more I realized I hadn't heard Smokie's mouth in a while either. As I walked through the kitchen, I had to push passed the people that were in there talking and dancing. I worked my way through the dining room to the entertainment room. Now I was really baffled because I really couldn't find Sharrin anywhere. I walked out to the patio and there she was dancing with Smokie. A very slow song was playing and they appeared to be doing more talking than dancing. I would never have guessed it, Smokie and Sharrin? Now that I had seen her, I started looking for Julian because I hadn't seen him in a while either. When I went back into the house I ran into Macy Gray talking to Tank, so I asked if she had seen Julian.

The music was loud, so she yelled a little. "Yeah, about 10 or 15 minutes ago he was headed upstairs and some woman was right behind him. You better go get your man, girl."

"Okay, thanks."

Julian's bedroom door was open so I walked right in. Camilla was lying on the bed and Julian was leaning up against his dresser, calmly talking to her.

"Camilla, you need to either leave the room or leave the house. Why do we have to go through this?"

I walked over to Julian and stood next to him. "Is everything okay?"

He stood up straight and put his arm around me. "Hey babe, I was just telling Camilla she needed to leave."

I looked at him and motioned for the glass of wine in his hand. I took a sip from it and stared at Camilla. "Look, dear, I can understand you still wanting to be with Julian, but he's with me now and I don't appreciate that every time I turn around you're up in his face. So, you really need to take Julian's suggestion and leave. I personally think he's being too kind, by giving you a choice, but since this isn't my home, yet, there's not much I can say about it."

Julian didn't interrupt me. He merely stood by and watched and listened. When I finished I took another sip from his glass and handed it back to him. Camilla slowly got up, rolled her eyes at me, and started walking towards the bedroom door.

As she brushed passed me she stopped and turned around. "Julian, I'm sure I'll talk with you later. You're going to have to tell her about us sooner or later. You might as well tell her now." She dramatically slammed the door behind her as she left the room.

Julian put his glass down and stood in front of me. He placed his hands on the dresser on either side of me. "I like the way you took control. It let's me know that you care…and it was kind of sexy."

I looked up at him. "So, what was she talking about? What is it that you need to tell me?"

He laughed as he started kissing my face. "Nothing. She was just trying to stir you up. That's how she works. If she can keep you mad at me then she figures she has a chance. Don't fall for it."

He kissed me on my forehead then my eyes, and then my cheeks, and my neck. He made a trail of kisses down to the top of my chest. Then he stopped and kissed me on my lips. He grabbed me by my waist. The next thing I knew he was picking me up and putting me on the bed. I didn't resist. Maybe this was what I had to do to keep him away from Camilla. I found myself anchored down by the weight of his body on top of mine. The heat that I felt coming from his body was feverish. The smell of his cologne alone was about to drive me out of my mind. I was just a little bit too involved to stop now. I didn't want to stop. Somehow, I managed to roll over on top of him. I straddled him and started unbuttoning his shirt and kissing his face, his neck, his chest. As I kissed him

I could feel his hands on my thighs, pushing my dress higher and higher up my legs.

I whispered in his ear. "I want you to make love to me so bad I could scream."

"Me too."

I started unbuckling his belt. At that very moment there was a loud knock and the door flew open. It was Kari. It hadn't occurred to me or Julian that the door was unlocked.

"Excuse me, I don't know if either of you is aware of it, but there's a party going on downstairs and, if I'm not mistaken, Julian is the host. He may want to come downstairs and entertain his other guests, too."

Kari walked out and left the door open. I stopped and rested my forehead on Julian's chin. I took a deep breath and dismounted him. I straightened out my dress and my hair and stood there looking at him pensively.

Julian lie there for a moment then he took his hands and wiped his face. "You know you're going to drive me crazy, right? I can't take this. I can't take it." He sat up on the side of the bed and buttoned his shirt then he stood up, tucked his shirt back into his pants, and buckled his belt.

Julian went back downstairs to the party. I went to my room, locked the door behind me, took a shower, and went to bed. He said I was going to drive him crazy. How did he think I felt? We were just minutes away from having sex. My head was still reeling. *This has got to stop. This madness has got to stop—I know it's me, but sometimes I get so caught up in the moment.* I grabbed the remote and jumped in the bed. It was about 3:45 and I mindlessly flipped through the channels, but I couldn't find anything on TV that I wanted to watch. There was a knock at the door, so I got up and unlocked it. It was Kari. She came in and shut the door behind her.

"What were you thinking about...getting busy with Julian with a house full of people downstairs? And to top it off, you don't even bother to lock the door. I wouldn't have thought anything about not seeing you, but some half-naked woman walked by me and was telling somebody that she was leaving and that Julian was up in his bedroom with 'what's her name.' I assumed she was referring to you. I wasn't sure. Look, Shelby, what you do is your business, but at least have some self-respect. And, anyway, I thought you were celibate?"

I sat down on the bed and looked at her. "First of all, Kari, you're right, you're right." I nodded my head as I spoke. "It is my business. You know, we were not having sex. We just got caught up in the moment. I mean, I think we both had a little bit too much to drink or something. I don't know." I looked down at the floor. "Kari, I love him so much that it's driving me crazy. I want to make love to him, but I want to wait, too.

Can I tell you something? The truth is, I almost had sex with him tonight because I thought it might be what I needed to do to keep him away from Camilla, that half-naked woman you saw."

Kari shook her head. "Please, you sound like a teenager. You know it doesn't work like that. Just from the little bit of time that I've spent with Julian, I can tell that man loves you, but you can't keep teasing him. He is a man. The next time there might not be anybody around to open the door." She worked her neck and looked me up and down. "You should also be worried about him easing his frustrations elsewhere. Know what I mean? Don't let that 'hoochie' get to you. Sex is obviously all she has to offer. Anybody could tell that by the way she was dressed.

I'm going back downstairs for a little while longer, and then I'm coming back up to go to bed myself. Since the kids aren't here I can stay up as late as I want to tonight and sleep as late as I want to tomorrow. You gonna' be all right?"

I nodded my head.

As she walked out the door, she turned back around. "You know I'm not trying to be in your business, but you know me."

I smiled as she closed the door.

Just as I was about to doze off, there was another knock at the door. I hadn't bothered to get up and lock it after Kari left, so I didn't bother getting up to answer it either.

"Come in." I sat up in the bed.

Julian stuck his head in. "Are you awake?"

"Uh, huh."

He came in and sat on the bed next to me. "Look Shelby, I need to understand something? I know we've already talked about this, but...are we or are we not going to make love? I'm only asking because I keep getting mixed messages from you. I mean, even though I think I know what you want to do, don't want to do, whatever. I just need for you to help me understand, one more time, where we're at with this."

I sat straight up now. "Nothing has changed. I still want to wait. I just think we both had a little too much to drink tonight and just got caught up in the moment." I shook my head because I wasn't sure my thoughts were being expressed clearly.

"So let me get this straight. You're saying the only reason you were sitting on top of me unfastening my belt was because we were drunk?" He kind of chuckled to himself. "I don't know what's up with you, but I'm crazy in love with you, girl, and I want to make love… to you."

"Exactly, what are you trying to say, Julian?"

"Shelby, you're a grown woman. You know you want to make love to me just as much as I want to make love to you. You've told me before and you made it pretty clear tonight, but you're sitting here acting like the only reason you were on top of me was because you had a little too much to drink. What's up with that, baby?"

I was so mad I thought I was going to pop, but I stayed calm. "I never said I didn't want to have sex with you, Julian. And you're right, I want to do it just as much as you do, maybe even more, but, in spite of how it looks, it's important to me…to wait. I'm not some 'freak' like your girl Camilla. I want to make sure we're going to be together, monogamously. This punanny is not free for the taking just because I care about you."

Julian stood up. "You say the word sex like it's bad or something. What's up with that? And you know what else? I don't understand why you would think our relationship was anything other than monogamous. Look, I'm not a little boy. I haven't been a boy in a long time. We can't keep playing this game." He paused for a minute. "Maybe I should make it clear. We are not going to keep playing this game. And, by the way, this has nothing to do with Camilla, this is about you and me."

He said what he had to say then turned and walked out of the room. While I was still sitting there with my mouth open, Julian stuck his head back in the door.

"You need to keep this door locked until everybody's gone." He locked the door and closed it behind him.

# Chapter 15

The rest of the weekend was pretty uneventful. Saturday everybody slept late. When we finally got up, Smokie and Julian fixed brunch for us. It was a pleasant surprise. After we ate, we spent the day watching movies and sitting around the pool talking. We took it easy and hung out all day Saturday. Sharrin and Smokie seemed to have a lot to talk about. Me and Julian, not so much. He was very quiet and standoffish, so I didn't bother him. He managed to find things around the house to keep himself busy, and away from me.

Kari and Sharrin's flight was leaving Sunday afternoon, so after getting up and getting dressed, we packed, had breakfast, and all the girls, including Kyomi and Tracie, prepared to leave. There was no shortage of hugs before we left.

"Not sure what's going on with you and Julian, but if you both want to slip away for a few minutes, we have time. I'm sure Smokie would be glad to keep us occupied until y'all get back." Kari then walked over to Sharrin and Smokie.

I looked over at Julian and thought, *Just get this over with. You know he's not going to act crazy front of everyone.*

"Julian, would you come here for a second?"

He looked at me then said something to Kyomi and Tracie.

"Yeah, what's up?"

The way he looked at me as he walked over was so intense that I looked down at the floor just to break the gaze.

"Look, Julian, I know…" I shook my head. "I want to say something. I just don't know what to say."

He shrugged his shoulders. "What can be said that hasn't been said already, Shelby?"

He was right.

"Okay, I'll call you later then."

"Yeah, that's cool, and if I miss you, or something, I'll call you back."

We both stood there for a few seconds. I had the feeling all eyes in the room were on us, but I couldn't tell because my view was obscured by Julian standing in front of me.

"So, is it okay for us to hug?"

If that was a low blow, I think I deserved it.

"Sure, yeah, let's do this so I can get my sisters to the airport."

Even though his words were cold, the way he held me was anything but. I smiled.

When Julian released his embrace he stepped back and gazed at me for a second. "Come on, y'all got to get to the airport."

Julian grabbed my hand as he escorted us out the kitchen door to our cars.

This time, he and Smokie watched as we drove down the drive.

The ride to the airport was quiet, until Kari spoke. "Is everything okay between you and Julian?"

I glanced over at her, and then turned my attention back to the road. "Of course it is, why wouldn't it be?"

"I don't know. This morning y'all just didn't seem as lovey-dovey as usual. As a matter of fact, y'all weren't that lovey-dovey yesterday either."

I smiled and quickly looked in the rearview mirror and looked at Sharrin in the back seat. "I think the more important question is, what's up with Sharrin and Smokie?"

Sharrin laughed. "He's a really nice guy. I mean, he's pretty deep, but nothing's up."

I just don't see it, but, then again, Smokie and I had never sat down and had an intelligent conversation.

When we arrived at the airport, I walked with my sisters as far as security would allow me to go. Kari talked about how she couldn't live in Julian's world because she couldn't party like that more than once a year. Of course, Sharrin was just the opposite. She would party like that every weekend if she could. It was nice to know they both had a good time. We said our goodbyes at the security checkpoint.

"Take care of yourself." Kari gave me a big hug.

"Thanks, girl. You got yourself an awesome man. Take it slow. I'll be calling you." Sharrin kissed me on the cheek and picked up her carryon bag.

It was kind of sad to see them go because now it was back to reality. Julian was going to be going on tour again in a few weeks, and Kari was right. Except, there was more than a little tension between me and Julian. Maybe time and distance would do us some good.

October rolled around very quickly and my relationship with Julian had been a little strained ever since the episode in his bedroom. We still talked every night and had dinner together as often as possible, but things were not quite the same. I figured it would blow over in a few more weeks. He was going to be leaving for a two and a half month concert tour and he hadn't invited me to attend any of the concerts this time, but I'm convinced the time apart will do us some good. In the back of my mind I keep hearing: *Distance makes the heart grow fonder or maybe out of sight out of mind.* I don't know.

Julian and I had dinner at his house the night before he left for his tour. Dinner was good, but conversation was very sparse. I would like to believe Julian had a lot on his mind. If Smokie hadn't shown up things may have gotten really uncomfortable. I have to give Smokie a lot of credit, he obviously sensed the mood when he walked into the room. I'm sure Julian had told him about what happened, so he knew what was going on. He didn't cut up like he usually did. At one point, while they talked, I cleared the kitchen table and loaded the dishwasher. Smokie was going on the tour with Julian, but, of course, he almost always traveled with him. They were going over a list of things that needed to be taken care of.

Smokie looked up at me. "Shelby, what shows will you need passes for?"

I quickly turned and looked at Smokie then at Julian.

"I don't think Shelby is going to be able to make it this time, man." Julian responded before I could say a word.

I continued to look at him. "Yeah, Julian's right. The kids are going to be getting out for the holiday in a little over a month, and then again in another month, so I need to be available. Maybe I'll be able to make it on the next tour."

In spite of what was said, Smokie didn't miss a beat. "I'll go ahead and save you two or three passes in the event you get a couple of free weekends."

At that moment I gained a newfound respect for him. Without even saying a word, he was telling me and Julian we needed to make the time to be together while Julian was away.

Julian called me at work from the airport, right before he boarded his plane. "Just wanted to hear your voice before I left. I also wanted to let you know, once I get settled, and you know that could take a couple of days, I'll call you. I love you, all right?"

I kind of smiled. "Okay, I'm going to miss you. Don't forget to call me."

"Okay, gotta' go, they're boarding the plane."

I didn't hear from him again for a little over two weeks. In a way, I was kind of glad he didn't call. It gave me a lot of time to think. I spent my time doing what I did best, hanging out with Kyomi and Tracie. We did a lot of talking and even spent a couple of weekends at Julian's house. I called Kari one night, just to hear the voice of reason. I really needed someone to tell me things were going to be okay. Who better than Kari?

"Hi Davis, is Kari home?"

"Hi, Shelby, how are you? Hold on for a minute. I'll get her.

For Davis, Kari's husband, we had just had an entire conversation. He's a man of very few words.

"What's wrong? Are you all right?"

I started laughing. "Geesh, Kari, of course I'm all right. Why would you ask me that?"

She calmed down. "Oh, okay. What do you want then?"

We both laughed. I loved my family's sick sense of humor.

"Do you remember that weekend you and Sharrin were here?"

"Of course, yeah. Most fun I've had in a long time. Uh, huh."

"Well, things have been different between us, me and Julian, ever since then."

"I knew it. What do you mean different?"

Now I almost felt silly calling her to whine. "There's been a lot of tension between us. He and I haven't talked about it because we know why it's there." I stopped for just a second to gather my thoughts. "Do you think I messed up?"

Kari didn't say anything for a minute. "Shelby, do you really love Julian?"

Before responding I pulled the phone away from my ear and looked at it. "Of course I do."

"Have you ever told him that?"

It didn't take me long to see where she was going. "No, I haven't."

"Then how is he supposed to know it? We've already determined that you're not sixteen years old. Stop acting like this relationship stuff is brand new to you. I mean, really, you were a married woman just a few years ago. You want to hear him tell you that he loves you; don't you think he wants to hear that from you, too? He's used to women throwing sex at him and calling it love. The fact that you've gotten this beautiful man to agree to wait until you're married to have sex is wonderful, but you have to let him know that you love him, Shell. You have to tell him. When did you get like this? What are you so afraid of?"

I knew it was a good idea to call her. The real question is: What am I afraid of? Whatever it is, I have to figure it out and fix it before I lose him.

When I finally heard from Julian his voice sounded like music to my ears.

"Hey, baby, it's me."

"I can't stay on the line long, I'm expecting a call from my boyfriend any minute now."

He laughed. That was a good sign.

"So, how's the tour going? Any good groupie stories for me?"

He laughed again, "Nope. Things have been pretty sane." He was quiet for a moment. "Shelby, I miss you, girl. I want to apologize for the way I was acting before I left. There was no excuse for me leaving things with you like I did...I'm sorry."

I thought, *If I can't tell this man that I love him then I'm crazy.*

"I owe you and apology, too, Julian. I know we should have talked before you left, but I don't know. I just didn't know what to say, and I didn't want to say the same old thing again. So, I'm sorry, too."

This man was going to be my husband and I knew it. We are soul mates. There was absolutely no reason why I shouldn't trust that he'll do the right thing with my love.

"Shelby, what are you doing, watching TV? Did you hear what I just said?"

"I'm sorry, baby, my mind wandered for a minute. What did you say?"

"I was just saying that I loved you and I really want to see you."

"That is so sweet. That's why I love you."

"Excuse me, did you just say you loved me?"

It felt so good, I said it again. "Yeah, I said I love you, boy. I…love…you."

There was silence.

"Are you still there?"

"Yeah, uhm, man. Look, let me know if you can fly here this weekend. If you can't that's okay, we'll do something special when I get back."

"Okay…"

Okay, so I did it. I told Julian that I loved him. For me, this meant we had taken our relationship to the next level. I told Tracie and Kyomi about my conversation with him. They were glad I finally admitted I loved him.

"So, now what? I know you weren't surprised by his response. I mean, it has been a whole year. How much longer did you think you could have gone without saying something?" Kyomi sucked her teeth as if she had just finished eating a piece of meat.

Tracie seemed to chuckle at nothing in particular. "Girl, stop acting like you didn't know he was going to be surprised. You scare me sometimes."

I didn't tell them about the real surprise I was going to have waiting at Julian's house when he got back. I had Smokie's cell phone number, so I decided to call him and find out exactly when they were coming back. Of course, I already had a key and the security code to Julian's house, so it wouldn't be a problem getting in the house. It was going to be nice waking up in his arms, after spending the night with him. How much more special could I make his return home?

Smokie eventually returned my call—three days later. He said he was busy, so many groupies, so little time. I don't know why I expected anything different. I guess he turns the charm on and off like a light switch.

"Shelby, look, before we start talking about you and Julian, would you do me a favor and call that fine sister of yours and have her waiting for me when I get back?"

"Boy, you are sick." Just when I thought I was going to have to give up on him he started talking like a human being.

"Look, Shelby, all jokes aside. I'm glad you and my boy handled your business. He ain't right without you. You got to be the one. I know it's hard to take me seriously most of the time, but Ju'man is like my brother. Don't hurt my boy, all right?"

His sudden display of emotions and the sincerity in his voice took me by surprise. "All right, Smokie, you have my word." I suddenly began feeling especially warm and fuzzy. "If you want me to, I'll call Sharrin and tell her you have a round-trip ticket at the airport for her, her own suite at the hotel where you're staying, and a backstage pass to the next Saturday night concert."

"Are you serious? Look here, you don't have to worry, I'm going to take good care of your people." His voice became muffled, like he had his hand over the phone. "Hey, I have to go, but we'll be back on December 23$^{rd}$. Anything you want me to tell Ju'man?"

"Uh, uh, no, that was really it, thanks."

149

The timing was pretty good because school would be out, so I didn't have to worry about leaving Julian's house early the next morning or asking for the day off.

It was difficult keeping my plans secret from everybody—especially Tracie and Kyomi because they keep asking me what I'm going to do for him when he gets back. Even Sharrin wanted to know if I was planning a party for him. The concert was getting really positive reviews in every city it played, so everybody was expecting me to throw a welcome home party for Julian, but I wanted to spend some quiet time with him first. The weeks before he left were terrible for both of us, so I really didn't want to share him with anybody as soon as he gets back. I was going to wait a week after the tour ended, and then Smokie and I could put our heads together and throw a little something together, but not before then.

Though Smokie gave me a general idea when Julian would get back, I didn't know what time his flight would be arriving. I suspect he'll come in on a late flight like he usually does. My initial plan was to pickup some scented candles and  splurge on a bottle of Cristal, that I really couldn't afford. Then it occurred to me to check Julian's bar and his pantry. I was sure he had at least one bottle somewhere around the house. After all, it's a special occasion, and special occasions should be celebrated with champagne. Rather than go to the grocery store, I was going to go through Julian's refrigerator for fruit and other things we could snack on. The mood music, it would come straight from Julian's

CD collection. And, yeah, what would the moment be without stopping by Vickie's Secret to get something sexy. *It's all in the presentation.* I laughed out loud because I knew it wasn't like I'd have the lingerie on long enough for it to matter. Before I forget, I also have to make sure to ask Smokie to get Julian to come straight home from the airport.

I was going to go by a florist to get some flower petals to throw on the bed, but that's was a bit overkill. Once my plan was in place, I met Kyomi at Tracie's house for dinner. We spent most of the evening talking about Julian and the party they thought I should have for him—because they felt like a party. I assured them there would be a party in a week or so.

At one point, during dinner, I noticed Tracie looking at me. "Why are you watching me for?"

"What's wrong with you, your mind has been somewhere else all night?"

I smiled then wrinkled my brow. "My man is coming home tonight and I haven't seen him in weeks. Can't I be a little excited about that?"

Kyomi laughed. "She wouldn't know, she doesn't have a man."

I think I laughed a little harder than usual.

"That's okay, y'all can laugh at me now, but when I do get a man I don't want y'all to be mad when I don't have time for y'all." Tracie waived her hand through the air and rolled her eyes.

I was absolutely giddy. Kyomi and Tracie thought I was tickled over our conversation, but I was ready for dinner to end, so that I could get everything set up at Julian's house. By the time we finished dinner, cleaned up, and talked a little while, it was after 9:00 p.m. That was actually good timing because it would give me plenty of time to drive across town.

# Chapter 16

The plan was to arrive at Julian's around 10:00 o'clock, to put the Cristal on ice and to take a shower by 11:00 pm. Julian should walk through the back door sometime between midnight and 1:00 in the morning. I bit my bottom lip as I considered how well planned things were.

When I arrived at Julian's house, I was so nervous I couldn't remember the code for the security gate, so I parked up front. I could come back out later and move my car. I put my suitcase next to the stairwell after I let myself in. I then went to the kitchen to cut up a little fruit and to put the champagne on ice. It took me about ten minutes to find what I was looking for. After I prepared a small tray of fruit I put it in the refrigerator and went back to the foyer to grab my suitcase. I headed for Julian's bedroom thinking, *I can't believe this is finally going to happen*. The timing was right and I was absolutely positive this would be the last thing Julian would expect.

As I approached Julian's room I noticed the door was slightly ajar and I thought, *That's weird. Why is his bedroom door closed, none of the others are?* I slowly pushed the door open. The only thing I could see was the big butt of a woman, in a thong, on all fours, straddling someone on the bed. A man's hands were on the woman's waist. The hands looked like Julian's, but how was that possible? Julian wasn't back yet. As my mind attempted to process what was going on, the woman began speaking.

"Julian, just relax, let me do this. It'll be like old times."

I immediately stepped back from the door. I think I pulled it closed; I don't know. I wanted to get out of the house as quickly as possible, but my feet wouldn't move. I slowly backed away from the door. The walk from the bedroom to the staircase had never taken as long as it was taking this night. Once I reached the stairs I turned and looked back one more time. Was it possible that my eyes and ears had deceived me? How could this be happening?

When I finally reached my car, I got in and sat there for a moment. I don't know how long. I felt sick to my stomach, but I couldn't cry. I didn't look back as I drove away. I couldn't believe Julian would do this to me. I had been such a fool. I was about to give this man the most precious thing I had...and he was having sex with someone else. All that talk. Like, something was wrong with me for wanting to wait until I was married. I felt like a fool. I couldn't go home because he would eventually call me and I didn't even want to be there when the phone rang, and I certainly didn't want to be there if he showed up. So, I decided to call Kyomi and ask if I could come over there. My hands were shaking, I pulled off the highway to call her, and to throw up.

"Kyomi, this is Shelby—"

Kyomi wasn't quite awake, but she could sense that something was wrong. "Shelby, what are you doing calling so late? Are you all right?"

I didn't want to tell her what had just happened, but I had to tell her something. "Look, things didn't go down tonight like I had planned, but I don't want to talk about it right now. I need somewhere to stay for a few days."

"Yeah, of course. Come on over." Concern was in her voice, but she didn't pry.

I made it to Kyomi's duplex in one piece. I couldn't remember anything about the ride from Julian's house to her house. It was like I had driven with my eyes closed. I sat in front of her place for a few minutes to gather my thoughts and to regain some semblance of composure. The night had drained me physically and mentally. I took a deep breath as I grabbed my suitcase and headed for the door. I felt silly for even imposing on Kyomi so late at night, but what are friends for? And after a few days at her house, then what? I don't know. It was kind of silly, but I really didn't know.

When Kyomi opened the door she was wide-awake. She stood to one side so I could walk in. "Come on in, unless you want to stand out there a little longer."

I looked at her. I didn't feel like responding, so I offered her all I had—a half smile.

Kyomi closed the door behind me. "Okay, do you want to tell me what's going on? What are you doing out roaming the streets this time of night? Is Julian all right?"

I shook my head. "Kyomi, I really just want to go to bed."

Kyomi put her hands on her hips and sighed. "Well, you know where the room is. Have a good night."

I don't think I ever slept. I laid there most of the night trying to make sense of what I saw. I think it was around 7:30 in the morning when Kyomi knocked on the bedroom door.

"Come on in."

She sat at the foot of the bed. "Good morning. You look terrible. Have you been up all night?"

"Thanks and good morning to you too." I knew I had to look a mess, so I laughed out loud.

Kyomi smiled at me. "But seriously, are you okay? What happened last night?"

Tears welled up in my eyes as I looked at her. "Kyomi, I'm just not ready to talk about it yet."

She nodded her head and pursed her lips. "Okay, you know I'm here for you when you're ready to talk about it."

I smiled. "I know. Thank you."

Kyomi gave me a hug. "Do you want anything for breakfast?"

My friend doesn't cook, so I was impressed that she was going to be such a good hostess. "I must look pretty darn bad for you to offer to cook breakfast for me."

Kyomi stood up and put her hands on her hips. "Girl, I'm offering to pick up something for you from McDonalds. You don't look bad enough for me to cook."

During the evening we caught up with Tracie and went to the beach, not to swim, just to walk around and talk. The best time to be at the beach is in the evening, right when the sun is setting and a light breeze is blowing. Every problem in life seems to wash away with the tide. A slow walk down the beach or even lying wrapped up in a blanket on a lounge chair, listening to waves, makes you feel better.

Of course, being at the beach on this particular day made me think about the first time Julian surprised me. I smiled as I recalled how he came to my house and picked me up for a romantic evening, after ignoring everything I had said to him earlier in the day about not wanting to get involved in a relationship with him. So, today I'm left wondering: *Why didn't I see it? I mean, I'm not that green. Well, at least I didn't think I was that green.* I felt a lone tear roll down my cheek. Tracie must have seen it, too.

"You okay?"

I looked over at her and shook my head. "No, but I will be."

We stayed at the beach for a couple of hours before deciding to head home. While we were there I made up my mind to take that trip home, by myself, to spend some time with my family. That would help me get my head straight. When we got back to Kyomi's house I immediately excused myself and took a shower and went to bed.

Late Sunday afternoon, I finally turned my cell phone on to check my voicemail messages, but only after Kyomi asked me, for the third time, if I had talked with Julian. I was kind of hesitant about checking voicemail because I knew he had probably called and left several messages. Just as I had expected, I had 18 messages—all from him. I received ten on Saturday and, so far, today I have received eight more. In the last message he said he was really worried about me, that he thought maybe I had gone out of town, but he wasn't sure and he didn't want to call my family and worry them, in the event I wasn't there. He also said he hadn't slept all night. *I bet.* After listening to my messages all I could do was close my eyes and shake my head. Kyomi must have been watching me.

"Girl, you all right? Is Julian back in town? What?"

I looked at her. I'm sure I looked a mess. "Yeah...he's back. I...I won't be seeing him anymore, though."

Kyomi looked at me. "What do you mean you won't be seeing him anymore? Didn't y'all make up?"

"He's been seeing somebody else." As soon as the words escaped my lips the floodgates opened and I started crying.

"What?" She walked over to me and grabbed my arm. "Shelby, I don't understand? Why would you think something like that?"

"I caught him having sex with her. I saw him with my own eyes...in his bed." I was now sobbing uncontrollably. I glanced up at Kyomi and she had tears in her eyes, too.

"Shelby, I'm so sorry...are you sure, though? Maybe it was Smokie. You know how Julian is about letting other people use his house when he's not in town."

I closed my eyes. "It was that same girl, Camilla. I heard her voice and I saw her naked butt in bed with him, saying his name, touching him."

"What are you gonna do?" Kyomi's words were little more than a whisper.

For now, the tears had stopped. I looked down at my hands. "I don't know. I just don't know. Well, yeah, I do. Of course I'm not going to see him anymore. I don't want to talk with him either. I told this man I loved him, Kyomi. For me—I guess for anybody—that's huge." I paused. Shaking my head, I continued. "I feel like such a fool. Like I was some kind of challenge for him...a game. He was only trying to wait me out, hoping that I would give in and have sex with him, and then he could put another notch on his belt. Ole' smooth Jules Brishard almost got me, too."

"What do you mean?" Baffled, Kyomi looked at me.

Holding my hand over my mouth, I smiled and shook my head. "Oh, yeah, I forgot, you don't know. I had a grand surprise all lined up for Mr. Brishard when he got back. I bought a couple of outfits from Victoria's Secret, had us some fruit all sliced up, and a bottle of Cristal on ice." I shook my head. "Hmph, I'm so silly. I had it all planned. I was going to stay with him for the entire weekend. I guess this is what I get for compromising something important to me for a man. I wanted to wait, but I figured we could go ahead and have sex. What would it hurt? We love each other, right? We were going to get married, right?

I guess it's better that I found out about things now, rather than later." I crossed my arms across my chest as I squinted my eyes and gazed at Kyomi. "I saw them in bed together. I opened the door...and I saw this naked woman on top of Julian, and he had his hands all over her."

Slowly shaking her head from side-to-side, Kyomi sat there dumbfounded. She never said another word. What was there to say?

# Chapter 17

To completely avoid Julian, I decided to visit my family. I knew I could clear my head at home with my family. The only problem I foresaw was Coco. He talked with Julian pretty regularly and I didn't want him to tell Julian I was there. I would just have to figure out a story to tell Coco.

The quicker I got home the better. Stepping off of the airplane was like a sigh of relieve, but it wasn't until I pulled into the driveway in my rental car that I actually felt as though a weight had been lifted off my shoulders. As I got out of the car to open the gate, I looked around for the dogs. My mom and dad have two dogs, which are part of a menagerie that also includes two cats, four exotic birds, and a 250 gallon fish tank filled with saltwater fish. They both love animals. I hadn't told anybody I was coming, so nobody was expecting me. When I pulled up to the garage I blew my horn a couple of times. My mom hated that, so I knew she would look outside.

As soon as she saw me she raced to the car and greeted me with a big ole, mama hug. "I told you about surprising us, baby."

"Well, I was coming home in a couple of days anyway, but I was able to get away a little sooner than I had originally planned."

My mom hugged me again. "I'm glad your plans changed. How long are you going to be here?"

I smiled. "You're going to have to deal with me the whole week."

"A whole week, huh?" Mom escorted me in the house.

I went to my old bedroom and sat on the bed before I unpacked my suitcase. I looked around the room and tried to remember how I used to feel as a teenager, when I had problems. Nothing like now. I also remembered how my sisters and I would get together in the room and talk about everything: school, teachers, clothes, boys, love, what our husbands were going to be like, how many children we were going to have, everything. Those were the days. Our expectations were pretty unrealistic. Well, Kari's weren't so unrealistic.

Her plan was always to, first, go to college and get her Masters in Elementary Education. She was going to meet her husband in college, or soon thereafter, and then she was going to date him for two or three years. She was then going to work a few years and by the time she was 29 or 30 she planned on being married. She would quickly have two children, and then be a stay at home mom until she was 40. I guess being the oldest child made her more organized and more in tune with everything. I don't really know what it is but Kari's life is right on track, just like she planned it when we were kids.

Sharrin, on the other hand, has not only always been impetuous and impractical, she has always wanted to live a very lavish lifestyle. She dated the best looking guy in high school, and they ended up being the cutest couple in their graduating class. When she went to college she dated the finest and, possibly, the wealthiest guy on campus. Her plan was plain and simple: She was going to marry rich and good looking. Of course, she went to college so that she could get a job to support her spending habits. Surprisingly, after college her ideas about life and marriage changed. She doesn't care about getting married anymore because she does quite well as a public relations director and she spends a lot of time partying and dating. The last time we talked about it, she figured she might consider getting married when she's about 40 yrs old, or so.

Then there's me…

Before I could finish my thought, my mom walked in. "You all right, baby? You look kind of funny."

I smiled at her. "I'm fine, Mom."

She sat down on the bed next to me and put her hand on top of mine. "I mean, are…you…all right?"

"I'm fine." I hung my head to one side and looked at her.

"Julian called last night." This time my mom smiled. "Coleman wasn't here, so he talked with me for a little while. He said he hadn't talked with you since he got back to town. He's worried about you, but he didn't want to worry us. He thought you might have told him your plans about going out of town and he forgot. So, I'm going to ask you one more time, are you all right?"

I grinned at her and sighed. "No, not really, but I'll be okay."

"I'm not going to ask you what's going on, but if you want to talk I'll be glad to listen." She squeezed my hand as she stood up. "There is one thing I'm going to say, though. He's not perfect, but neither are you. Remember that."

My mom walked out of the room, but her words lingered long after she was gone. I do love Julian, but how could I forgive infidelity? Better yet, how could I forget it? My mom came from a different school of thought. I think women her age tolerated a lot more than women my age would ever dream of putting up with. I don't want to be married to someone I have to tolerate. I want to be married to someone I can trust.

When Coco got home he hugged me and asked about Julian. It annoyed me that he was so fascinated with someone I was dating, but I knew the truth was it wasn't so much that he was fascinated with him, as much as he was fascinated with his lifestyle. I also knew I was only aggravated because I was mad with Julian.

"I'm fine, my trip was fine, and I'll be here for about a week. How's Coco doing?"

He laughed because he knew I was being sarcastic. He hadn't asked me how I was doing or anything.

"What are you tripping about? Did Julian tell you I was going to be up there for New Years Eve?"

"No, he didn't. He docsn't tell me everything." I tried to sound as unconcerned as possible.

Coco still wasn't getting it because he seemed to think he and I could fly back together. I had to deflate his plans because I wasn't going back until after New Years Day. That was the end of our conversation. He had to go make other plans.

When my daddy got home he kissed me on my forehead and asked how I was doing, as he walked through the family room to his bedroom. He stopped and stood in front of me when he came back through the room to get his dinner.

"So, what's going on with you and the singer guy? Your mom told me he called last night. Y'all had a fight?"

My daddy is a very sweet and intelligent man, but tact has never been his forte. When we were growing up he was always asking us embarrassingly direct questions. It's a wonder my sisters and I aren't more self-conscious. My brothers were never phased by anything he said, though. I got up and followed him into the kitchen.

"No, we haven't had a fight. Why would you even ask me that, Daddy?"

As he walked past me, into the kitchen, my daddy turned around and looked at me. "Because you're here…without him."

I left my dad alone after that.

My first night at home was exactly what I expected: chit-chat and questions. I called Sharrin and Kari to make arrangements to spend one night with each one of them. Even though we talked on the phone often, I still missed doing 'sister stuff.'

My mom and I spent my second day in town out and about because she felt the need to dedicate a whole day to me. She seems to think the world of Julian, even though she hasn't officially met him yet. Apparently, the reports from my siblings have impressed her enough for her to give him her seal of approval. She really wanted me to give him a chance, and she wasn't interested in what he had done because, to her, it was irrelevant. According to my mom, part of loving someone is overlooking their faults and helping them to work on overcoming them. Mom assured me that all of her children have faults, and she expects the people that love them to work through her children's problems with them because it's not her job to do that anymore.

She is certainly a great lady, and not just because she's my mother. She and my dad raised us to be thinkers, so I guess I should spend less time feeling sorry for myself and more time thinking about a resolution to my problem.

I spent my first night out at Sharrin's ultimate chick, very art deco house. She also has the ultimate view of the ocean. After we came back from dinner, which we had to go out for because Sharrin doesn't cook, we sat up most of the night talking. It seemed like she had been thinking about Smokie a lot. Several time during our conversation, she kept referring to "Omar." At first, I thought this Omar was a new guy she was seeing. You never know with her, but a couple of times she said something about 'the concert.'

I was tired of trying to figure it out. "Who is Omar? He must have really put the whammy on you."

Sharrin looked at me, clearly puzzled. "I'm talking about Smokie."

I started laughing. "Smokie is an Omar? I would never have guessed that. He looks more like a Chris or an Antoine. Omar…wow."

I guess I must have touched a nerve.

"What do you mean by that?"

I smiled. "Mean by what? I didn't say anything."

Sharrin gazed at me. "I bet you've never even sat down and talked with Omar. He's a really, really nice guy. Obviously he's a little complicated because he's, you know, nothing like he appears to be. He's probably just as sweet as Julian. They're a lot alike, you know. That's one of the reasons they're so close."

I wonder what happened when she went to Julian's concert? It was apparent Smokie showed her a really good time and made a good impression on her. I've always considered her to be an excellent judge of character, even though she only goes for guys with really good looks, lots of money, and lots of personality. In the past, if they had any major character flaw, according to her, she had them out of the picture so quickly they didn't even know what hit them. In spite of that, they all remain friends with her. Well, I'm glad she spent some quality time with Smokie. I still haven't figured him out, but if she has, good for her.

I must have been lost in thought because as Sharrin was leaving the room I thought I heard her say Smokie had told her what was going on between me and Julian. I sat quietly and waited for her to come back in the room.

"What were you saying when you walked out? I thought you said something about me and Julian."

As she sat down, she sighed. "I did. I said Omar told me that something bad was going on between you and Julian. He's not sure what it is, but he knows you and Julian haven't seen each other since Julian got back in town. So, what's up with that?"

I sat there and looked at her for a few seconds because I didn't really know if I could tell her anything, now that she and Omar seemed to be so close. She might tell him, and, of course, he would go right back and tell Julian.

Instead, I made up something. "I finally realized Julian's lifestyle was too much for me. I'm just not sure how to tell him yet."

As weak as my story was, she looked convinced that I was telling the truth. Good for me because I wasn't in the mood to hear a lecture about Julian's virtues.

The next day, around mid-morning, I left for Kari's house. I hung out there doing kid stuff all day. When

Davis got home he didn't say very much. He ate his dinner, played with the kids, sat and talked with me for a few minutes, and then went to bed. Kari and I sat up until midnight talking about my ex-husband. She, along with everyone else, was still shocked by the fact that during our marriage Lorenz appeared to have himself together, even though he was really a closet alcoholic and a philanderer.

"I bet you there're a lot of people out there living double-lives. You think?"

Kari laughed. "I'd like to believe it's the exception rather than the rule."

*If that was truly the case, how is it that I had the dubious distinction of meeting two men in a row that did it?*

It was nice to spend a little time with Kari, so I never mentioned finding Julian in bed with Camilla. I knew Kari would give me some sound advice and a lot to think about, but I thought I would work this one out on my own.

When I got back to my mom and dad's place I found out Coco had talked with Julian and told him I was there, so I had a message to call him as soon as possible. I thought, *Great, now I have to call him.* I didn't know if I was ready for that, so I decided to call Julian right before I left the house for the airport—that way I could use my flight as an excuse to get off the phone. My plan was to arrange to meet Julian for dinner, right before I hung up the phone. I wouldn't have time to explain anything because of my flight. I could get back to my house and sit down and gather my thoughts before meeting up with him. I didn't get a chance to fuss at Coco because he had already left to attend the New Year's Eve party that Julian was either having or had been invited to.

I spent the last couple of days at home hanging out and talking with my mom and dad. Both of them kept reminding me to call my 'boyfriend.' The Friday, before I left, Sharrin, Kari, the kids, and Kristoff came over to have dinner and spend the night. We stayed up all night talking and playing cards. It was just like when we were kids.

I got up early the next morning because I couldn't sleep. My mom was up fixing breakfast for my dad, so I had breakfast with them. During breakfast my mom told me not to worry about things so much and my dad told me to be careful and to think before I act. It was almost like they knew what I was getting ready to do. I assured them I wouldn't do anything crazy, though. I didn't want them to worry about me. I was the only one of their children that didn't live within a 45 mile radius of them. As a matter of fact, I was the only one that didn't live in the same state. They very seldom knew what was going on with me, except for when one of my siblings happen to mention something. I knew they worried, but, at the same time, they also knew I could take care of myself.

My dad's solution to every problem I had was for me to get married again. It was apparent, he was hoping it would be Julian. Like everyone else, he was very fond of him too, in spite of having never met him. Didn't look like that was going to happen, though, and I was quickly becoming okay with that. I could think of worse things than not being Julian's wife.

As I got ready to leave for the airport, I called Julian. He answered on the first ring.

"Hello…"

I paused, and then quietly sighed. "Hi Julian. I got your message. Sorry for not calling before now."

"Girl, for a while I thought you had disappeared off the face of the earth. I apologize for calling your parents, but I got kind of worried." He sounded genuinely happy to hear from me." Crazy things happen all the time, so I just wanted to make sure nothing had happened to my baby."

"I'm okay. I can't really talk long because I'm on my way to the airport. After I get back, let's meet for dinner at Houston's downtown on Main Street. Is 6:30 okay?"

He agreed to meet me, so we hung up and I left for the airport. As I put the receiver on the hook I had a thought. I remember once telling Julian I believed we could work out any problem we would ever have. I guess I really didn't mean that. It sounded good at the time though. I absolutely dreaded leaving my family and going back to real life. Fortunately, school would be starting Monday, so work would keep me occupied.

My flight landed on time, so I went straight home and took a nap. When I woke up I still had a few hours before dinner, so I looked over some files that I had brought home from work. I couldn't concentrate, so I watched a little TV instead. I finally took a shower, got dressed and, at 5:45 p.m., left for the restaurant.

My intention was to get there early and have a drink, or two, to calm my nerves. I had been having anxiety attacks all day. I couldn't believe it was going to end like this. I still couldn't get over how wrong I had been about Julian. He seemed nice enough. Not perfect, but one of the good guys, for sure. Was it possible that it was somebody else in the bed? Maybe Camilla knew I was coming over and she set it up to look like she and Julian were having sex? But how would she know I was going to be there? I was beginning to unravel. I guess I was grasping for straws.

I saw Julian before he saw me. One thing sure hadn't changed, the boy looked good. As he approached the table he flashed one of his million dollar smiles. I managed to return a closed lip smile. He walked straight toward me and attempted to kiss me on the lips. Without even thinking about it, I turned my head and he kissed my cheek. He stepped back and looked at me.

"So, what's going on, Shelby? Where have you been for the last couple of weeks? I've been leaving messages for you all over town. I went by your condo and I even went by the school a few times, even though I knew it was closed."

I took a deep breath before I sipped on my glass of wine. I didn't look at him. I couldn't. "I've been doing a lot of thinking the last couple of weeks and I think, uhm, I think we need to slow things down. You know…with us." As I ran my finger around the rim of my glass, I looked up at Julian. "Maybe even consider seeing other people."

Julian sat back in his chair and squinted his eyes as he gazed at me from across the table.

He leaned forward, hands folded, his elbows on the table. "Where is all of this coming from, Shelby?"

I could barely look at him, partially because the last time I saw him—with the other woman—was still fresh in my mind and partially because I loved him so much.

"I know this relationship has been difficult for you, Julian…because we haven't been able to have sex…"

Julian stopped me. "This isn't about me. I can speak for myself. What's really up? I mean, what's going on, Shelby? Look, baby…" He leaned closer to me. "I don't know what's wrong, but we can fix it. You gotta' talk to me, though. You're coming out of left field with this. How long have you felt this way? Is it Smokie? What?"

I just wanted to get up and walk out. I wasn't going to lie to him and I couldn't believe he was sitting there acting like he didn't know what was going on. I guess the truth was, he didn't know. I saw him, he didn't see me. So, as far as he's concerned I don't know that he's been with someone else. I wonder if he's been with any other women or if he just split his time between me and Camilla?

I took a deep breath. "Look, let's just do this. You may not believe it right now, but it's the best thing…for both of us."

I had never seen Julian so crushed.

"Shelby, I can't read your mind, so I don't know what's going on right now. I'm kind of confused because I thought we loved each other? If it's somebody else, that's cool, but that's what you need to tell me. I'm not gonna lie, I feel like you just snatched my heart out and kicked it across the room...for no apparent reason.

When I first met you, you told me you didn't like to play games. Right now I'm feeling played. I want to beg you not to do this, but I'm not going to do that. I will say this, though. If I've done or said anything to hurt you then just tell me 'cause we can fix that. I can make that right. I love you, Shelby. You know that. I know you love me too, so don't do this." He stood up. "So this is it? It's over just like that, huh? You say it's over and it's just over, no explanation, nothing? You say it's the best thing for both of us and I'm supposed to take it like a man, I guess. What about the last few months, Shelby? Didn't they mean anything to you? If they didn't then you're a great actress, but I don't believe that."

Julian walked around the table, grabbed me by my shoulders and lifted me to my feet. He kissed me right there in front of everybody. When I opened my eyes he was standing there looking at me.

"Tell me 'that' didn't feel right."

I stood there and watched him as he turned and walked out of my life.

# Chapter 18

The school winter break has ended, so work has definitely kept my mind occupied during the day. I'm not concentrating very well, but it's keeping me busy, none-the-less. In spite of that, I periodically find myself going to the restroom to splash a little cold water on my face, after brief crying spells that seem to come from nowhere.

The nights have been much more difficult, though. When I'm home alone or when Tracie and Kyomi are busy, I'm finding it difficult not to pick up the phone to call Julian. I'm determined not to do it, though. I can't give in like that. At night, instead of sleeping, I find myself lying in bed thinking about the day we met. I think about that day at the beach, too; working out with him at his house; the times we almost made love; the time I told him I loved him. Sometimes I find myself smiling or even laughing out loud. The truth is, most of our time together was good...happy. Actually, all of our time together was good. I don't know what to think about that.

I am having a more difficult time with this breakup than I did with my divorce. What's up with that? I have never cried so much in my life. If things don't get any better I'm going to have to take a couple of vacation days at the end of the month to get myself together.

Fortunately, by the time February rolled around it seemed like the stream of tears had dried up. Julian was going to be on the music awards, and Kyomi and Tracie made sure I knew it. They invited themselves over to watch it at my house.

"...and the award for best new neo soul artist goes to...Jules Brishard for his CD, *Subtle Lover*."

Kyomi and Tracie clapped and screamed for him, but I sat and looked at the TV as he walked up to the stage to accept his award. It had been a little over two months since the last time I had seen him and he still looked good, real good. I smiled to myself. Images of him with his freak immediately crowded my thoughts. My smile didn't last long. I begin to feel a little sick to my stomach, so I got up to go into the kitchen.

Kyomi grabbed me by my hand as I was getting up. "You okay?"

I could have easily lied and said, yeah, I'm fine, but what was the point.

"No, I'm not all right, so I'm going to step out of the room for a minute, to get some fresh air and a glass of water or something."

In the background I could hear Julian thanking people. I heard him thanking his mom and grandma for all of their love and support. As I left the room, Kyomi looked at me with puppy dog eyes and asked me to stay until Julian was finished.

Suddenly Tracie hollered out. "Y'all listen...listen."

Julian was still on stage thanking people, or so I thought.

"None of this means anything if you don't have someone to share it with, so I'd like to dedicate this award to someone who means everything to me. I'd gladly give up all of this to have her back in my life. Shell, I love you."

Tracie and Kyomi turned and looked at me.

"Ooh, Shell, girl. He's talking about you." Tracie looked at me, and then back at the TV.

I heard him and I was very moved, but I wasn't going to cry in front of them. I was sick and tired of the tears.

Later, before Julian performed, he was introduced by the host, Chris Rock. The song Julian would be performing was a song off of his new CD titled *Feel Me?*. I sat back down to listen.

*I thought about you a lot today, couldn't get you off my mind*
*It seems like forever since I've seen you*
*When I lay down, put my head on the pillow, you were right there*
*Felt your breath on my cheek*
*I knew it was you because pictures of you went through my mind, and it felt good*

*It felt like you*
*Do you feel me when I see you in my dreams?*
*Did you feel me when our tongues touched?*
*What about when I held you in my arms?*
*Did you feel me when I looked at you and got drunk*
*off your love?*
*Do you feel me?*
*When I'm laughing with my boys I smile because I'm*
*thinking 'bout you*
*How you used to walk up behind me and put your*
*arms around me*
*How you danced when you walked*
*How you held me with the sparkle in your eyes*
*How your perfume demanded my attention...*
*and made me feel you*
*Do you feel me when I see you in my dreams?*
*Did you feel me when our tongues touched?*
*What about when I held you in my arms?*
*Did you feel me when I looked at you and got drunk*
*off your love?*
*Do you feel me?*
*It's no accident that I feel you*
*You let me in your love*
*And you captured my soul with your passion*
*So why can't you feel me?*
*I feel you, I feel you, I feel you*
*Do you feel me when I see you in my dreams?*
*Did you feel me when our tongues touched?*
*What about when I held you in my arms?*
*Did you feel me when I looked at you and got drunk*

*off your love?*
*Do you feel me?*
*Why can't you feel me?*

Kyomi looked over at me. "You know he's talking about you. Girl, call that man and give him an opportunity to explain what happened."

I looked at her, and then turned away.

As Kyomi and Tracie were leaving they both gave me hugs.

Kyomi whispered in my ear. "He loves you, Shelby. At least talk to him. I don't think he'd intentionally do anything to hurt you. He's not Lorenz. I'll call you tomorrow."

I looked at her and gave her a half smile. I appreciated and understood what she was saying, but it wasn't enough to change anything.

It was hard to get to sleep that night. I couldn't stop thinking about Julian or his song. He looked so good. The more I thought about him the more I realized how sad he looked. He looked like he'd lost a little weight too. He was wrong about one thing, I could definitely feel him.

I know what I saw that night and no one can convince me otherwise. Lorenz used to play head games like that with me all of the time. I'd get a hang up call, so I'd *69 it and the woman on the other end would say, "No one called from this number." I wouldn't even argue with her. I'd ask Lorenz to stop his friends from calling the house and hanging up. He would always get mad at me for calling them back. In addition to accusing me of making the whole thing up, he would tell me that I was paranoid.

When I confronted him with cards and pictures I found in the house, he'd say, "They're just friends, stop tripping. You're always trying to make something out of nothing."

I can still hear that condescending tone in his voice. "Stop trying to make something out of nothing…"

Lorenz was sleeping with so many women I couldn't keep count and now Julian's playing the same game, except I caught him in bed with his woman. And what do my friends say to me? The same thing Lorenz used to say, "You're making something out of nothing."

About three weeks after the awards show I came home to a voicemail message from Smokie. He said he would call me back later. *Oh, boy, Smokie's going to call me back. This is going to be interesting.* As strange as it may sound, I actually, kind of, missed talking with him. I knew he wanted to talk about Julian. He'd probably want to talk about Sharrin, too. I went into the bathroom, took off my workout clothes and jumped in the shower. Afterwards, I fixed myself something to eat. While I ate, I read over some information I had brought home from work. It was getting late and I still hadn't heard back from Smokie, so I went and got in the bed. I guess he decided not to call. I looked over at the clock on my nightstand; it was 11:00pm. I turned off the light and called it a night.

Of course, as soon as I closed my eyes the phone rang.

"Uhhh, hello."

"Hey, Shelby, this is Smokie. Sorry for calling so late. I just got off of the phone with Sharrin."

I smiled, "Oh, hey, Omar."

Smokie laughed, "Okay, I ain't mad at 'cha or your people because I know who told you my name. Look here, though. You know why I'm calling, it's about my man Julian. We've known each other since we were little fellas and I know him as well as I know myself. First, let me tell you, I'm breakin' all the rules by calling you, but my boy is hurtin' real bad right now. He says everything is all-good, but it's not. He told me how you felt about me, so I want to apologize to you because I didn't mean any harm. It's just my way of weedin' out the chicken heads. Julian has been all about you since day one, so I didn't want to see him get burnt. Know what I mean?

There are a lot of women out there who'd put on a good game face to be with my boy, but they ain't really 'bout nothing. They just want to be with 'Jules Brishard.' Know what I mean? They just want what goes along with the name—the glamour and the money. So, as his brother, it's my job to watch his back."

I sat up in the bed to listen more closely.

He continued. "I hate breakin' down and calling you, but it's either this or continue to deal with my man like he is. I can't keep watching him like this. It's a trip. He don't wanna eat. He's having a hard time sleepin'. He can't concentrate…you know what I'm talkin' about. If I have anything to do with you staying away then be mad at me, take it out on me, don't take it out on Julian."

He stopped talking, so I took that as my cue to say something.

"Smokie, please don't think that this whole thing is about you. Since you've been talking to my sister I've really come to realize that you aren't so bad after all. Really, this is bigger than how I've felt about you in the past. This is about me and Julian. How I feel about his lifestyle, how I feel about maintaining my own identity…"

Smokie interrupted. "I don't understand what you're saying. You gone have to explain that."

I took a deep breath. "I don't want to give up myself, what I believe is morally right or wrong, just to be with him. I mean, I don't want to find myself accepting behavior that I don't find acceptable in a relationship—a monogamous relationship—just because I want to be with him. I've never been one to settle."

Smokie stopped me again. "Okay…you know Julian is getting large and he has groupies everywhere he goes, but it's part of my job to keep them away from him, as much as possible. You know he has his head on straight. He ain't tryin' to get with none of them. My boy ain't that guy."

I couldn't believe Smokie and I were having a civilized conversation…about my relationship with Julian, his best friend. It would be good to get his perspective on things, but, at the same time, how could I really expect him to tell me the truth? He's looking out for Julian's best interest, not mine. It's difficult to think rationally when I'm so emotional. I really didn't mind talking with him, but before I say another word I had to know one something.

"Smokie, tell me one thing. Would you lie for Julian?"

He laughed. "Of course I would, if I had to, but I wouldn't lie to you."

That was not exactly what I was expecting to hear. Actually, I thought he would say no.

I grinned and shook my head. "Smokie…"

I guess I paused too long. "Shelby, you still there? What's wrong?"

I thought I could get through this conversation without getting emotional.

"Smokie, I really love Julian…I do, and I'm terrified. I don't want to be hurt again. It's too much. I want to trust him, but it's hard with women always wanting to…trying to be with him, and what about his ex-girlfriends? I don't want to compete for his love."

"Whoa, I can personally assure you, there is no competition. My boy loves you. As far as women go, it's only a couple that can truthfully say they were his lady. The others that he's gone out with were just for the night or the event…and I don't mean that in a bad way. Julian isn't like other brothers, he treats women good, sometimes too good, I think. So, you don't have to worry 'bout Julian messing 'round on ya'. Matter of fact, Julian has been played a time or two, himself."

I thought Smokie said he wouldn't lie to me, but he had done just that. Julian was with another woman. I know it because I saw it with my own two eyes and it made me mad that Smokie had the audacity to tell me Julian wouldn't cheat on me. Before I knew it, something came over me.

"How can you, in one breath, tell me you wouldn't lie to me and in the next breath do just that? You know, as well as I do, that y'all are so close that you would lie for him. You'll lie to anybody, including me, if you felt like you had to. Let me tell you something I know you don't know. When Julian came back from his last tour I wanted to surprise him. I wanted to do something really special for your friend, your brother. Do you remember me calling you and asking you, specifically, when Julian would be coming back? I wanted to be at his house when he got back. I wanted the night to be really, really special. If you know what I mean. You know what, though? I was the one that was surprised. So tell me this, Smokie, if he won't mess around on me, how is it that I caught him in bed with somebody else?"

For a few seconds there was silence. I sat there with my mouth open because I couldn't believe what I had just screamed. I couldn't even hear Smokie breathing. I sighed and closed my eyes.

Smokie finally spoke, a little softer and a little slower than before. "Shelby, I…this is… this is deep. I can't tell you what you saw or what you thought you saw, but I know Julian loves you and he wouldn't do anything to hurt you. He hasn't talked about anybody else since he met you. I can't tell you what you saw, but I think you should talk with him."

What was I supposed to say? The conversation was over. I caught him in a lie and he was stumped, speechless.

"Good night, Smokie."

"Good night…"

As I hung up, I heard his last word. "Deg."

# Chapter 19

After the awards show, not a day went by that Kyomi or Tracie didn't try to convince me to call Julian. I never told them about the conversation I had with Smokie. I was still a little bothered by it. Honestly, I had expected to hear from Julian by now. Instead, Sharrin called about a week after my conversation with Smokie.

"Omar called me after he talked with you. He was very upset and, for once in his life, at a loss for words. I promised him I wouldn't talk to you about it, so I'll only say, I think you should talk with Julian because it's possible things weren't exactly as they seemed."

"What do you mean by that?"

"That's all I can really tell you, Shell. I promised Omar I wouldn't tell you he and I talked. Just call Julian, okay?"

"We'll see."

Shortly after our conversation, I was tempted to call Julian. I actually picked up the phone, but each time I got a horrible feeling in the pit of my stomach, and I hung up.

On a Friday, about two weeks after my conversation with Smokie, I was about to call it a day at work. I was clearing off my desk when the phone rang.

"Denval Senior High, this is Ms. Simone."

For a brief moment there was silence. So I said it again. "Denval High, this is Ms. Simone. How may I help you?"

The voice on the other end sounded sweetly familiar. If I didn't know any better, I'd swear my heart actually skipped a couple of beats.

"Hi, Shelby, this is Julian. Please don't hang up."

"Okay."

He continued. "Wait a minute. I can't remember what I was going to say. It's good to hear your voice, though. Look, I called because I want to see you. I know we have some unresolved issues. I would like an opportunity to talk with you about everything. It would mean a lot to me if you would agree to meet me tomorrow night? Before you answer, I just want you to know that I won't call you anymore, if that's what you really want. I'll accept that it's over, but it would mean a lot to me if you would meet me for dinner. Maybe for what might be the last time that we'll ever see each other."

Just hearing his voice made my eyes fill with tears. I really wanted to see him too, and, he was right, it probably would be the last time we saw each other.

"Where do you want to meet?"

I could feel his smile through the telephone, so I smiled, too.

"Mr. Vestas will pick you up right after sunset, around 8:30 p.m. or 9:00 p.m. I can't wait to see you, baby. Thank you. I'll see you tomorrow night."

I said bye and we hung up.

Instead of rushing home and calling Kyomi and Tracie, I headed for the Galleria to get a new outfit. If this was going to be the last time we saw each other I wanted to be drop dead gorgeous.

I didn't stay in the mall long. I knew what I wanted, so I went in, looked for it, bought it, and then left. After I found my, "you gonna' be sorry you cheated on me, outfit," I stopped and grabbed a bite to eat, and then headed home. Once I got home I realized I was too nervous to eat, so I thought I'd relax by taking a bath. My bath relaxed me, but I couldn't go to sleep, so I watched music videos. Wouldn't you know it, one of Julian's videos came on. I smiled, turned the TV off, and went to bed.

The next day seemed to drag on and on. Kyomi and Tracie each had things to do, which was good for me because I didn't feel like hanging out anyway. I called my parents and talked with them for about an hour. Afterwards I had a conference call with my brothers and sisters. Talking with my family always puts me at ease. After getting off of the phone I felt ready to face the world.

The limousine arrived right after sunset, but, of course, in Shelby style, I wasn't ready. As I stood in front of the mirror I looked at myself from head to toe and thought, *I'm not going to cry tonight. I'm not going to cry.* I headed for the limo before I changed by mind. Once I was in the car, Mr. Vestas and I struck up a conversation. I hadn't seen him in a while and, of course, that was one of the first questions he asked me.

"Good to see you, Ms. Shelby. Where have you been? I haven't seen you around the house much lately. You know, I told Julian that I liked you when I first met you. That young man seems to have a good head on his shoulders, but he's still young. When I missed you coming around, one day I pulled him to the side and told him he better not let you get away because you are a 'keeper.' I'm just tellin' it like it is. Out of his few female friends that I've met, you have more respect about yourself than any of them. I mean that. Look at you, you're just beautiful. That boy better not act crazy, that's all I got to say…he better not act crazy."

I smiled and looked out the car window. "Thank you, you're too kind, Mr. Vestas. You must have known I needed to hear that."

"Uh, uh, I didn't know that, but it makes me feel good to tell the truth…sure do."

I continued to look out at the darkness as the trees and houses seemed to rush pass the car. "Where are we going, Mr. Vestas?"

"No, ma'am. I can't tell you that. And you might as well not ask me again. It's a surprise."

As I looked at his reflection in the rearview mirror, my curiosity was now piqued. Knowing Julian, it would probably be someplace romantic. Well, actually I didn't know that. I had already assumed to know him and look what that got me. I literally shook my head to shake the negative thoughts away. It could, very well, be someplace that has a lot of people and space because we haven't seen each other in months. Julian wouldn't want to appear to forward or anxious. Then again, maybe he chose a quaint, little secluded place, so we could talk with no interruptions.

While I was lost in thought, the car pulled into the driveway of the Victoria Botanical Gardens. I still couldn't figure out exactly what was going on. We drove all the way to the back of the property to the estate mansion on premises. Mr. Vestas proceeded to pull around to the side and park. Now I was truly baffled. I couldn't imagine why we were meeting here.

Mr. Vestas parked, exited the car, and opened my door.

"Thank you, Mr. Vestas. Where's Julian?" I stepped out and looked around.

Mr. Vestas pointed to his right and nodded his head in the same direction. "See that walkway a few feet away? You gone go down there then go through the gate. Once you go through the gate you should find your way all right." He then, very kindly, escorted me across the grass to the sidewalk. "You have a good night, Ms. Shelby. Okay?"

I turned and looked at him. "Okay…"

Approaching the gate, I could see candles going down both sides of the walkway. As I made my way through the garden, I reminded myself: *Remember, you're not going to cry*. I took a deep breath and continued to walk. What I saw was nothing short of breathtaking. I begin to feel like I was going to give in to whatever Julian asked. In spite of the fact that I thought I was approaching this night with an open mind, because I had taken a lot of time to think about everything that had been said to me in the past few weeks, I had come to the conclusion that, in part, everybody was right. I did need to listen to Julian's side.

Like Kyomi said, I shouldn't base my decision on what happened with Julian to anything that happened to me in my marriage. That was a different time, a different place, and definitely a different man. I needed to look at the history that Julian and I had created together, not the history that I had with my ex. As far as I was concerned, I'm going into this night completely objective…and totally emotional.

When I reached the end of the walk I could see a gazebo covered with a flowering vine. In the center of it sat a table with a setting for two. On the table was also the flicker from the flame of a single candle lit centerpiece. I must have gotten there a little faster than Julian had anticipated because I stood there and watched as he patted his jacket down. He looked like a nervous little high school boy waiting for his prom date to come into the room. *Goodness, he looked good*. I smiled when I realized my silk, off-white tank dress and gold sling-back platform sandals coordinated with his brown velvet blazer and off-white shirt with a raised print design.

When Julian finally looked up at me, the few seconds we stood there staring at each other felt like several minutes. After he came to his senses, he started walking towards me. He grabbed me so quickly that I didn't have time to react. I closed my eyes and held on, that was all I could do at the moment.

He whispered in my ear. "Thank you for coming, Shelby." When he released his embrace he stepped back. "You look beautiful."

I offered him a sincere smile that came from deep within my heart. "Thank you." I touched the lapel of his jacket. "Velvet, huh? I like."

His eyes smiled back at me.

Once we sat down, a waiter appeared from nowhere and quickly poured two glasses of wine. Five minutes later our first course was served. The most memorable part of our meal was dessert. I think that was by design because Julian knew I had a weakness for sweets. After the waiter removed our plates, Julian reached across the table and cupped my hands, which I had folded on the table in front of me. During the entire dinner we hadn't broached the incident that had brought us where we were tonight. Our dinner discussion had been more of a 'catch up' conversation, so it was about time for him to plead his case.

With his head slightly bowed and his eyes closed, he took my hands and put them up to his lips and kissed them softly. "Shelby, you know I love you. I love you more now because I know what it feels like to lose you. You told me once that I never had to swear to you because my word would always be enough." He opened his eyes and looked at me. "You have my word. I would never…do anything…to hurt you. I would rather hurt myself first.

Smokie told me what you saw. I'm telling you, Shelby, that night you walked into my bedroom and caught me in bed with another woman…nothing had happened, nothing was going to happen. That night I walked into my room, got undressed, and got straight into bed. The next thing I knew Camilla was crawling on top of me, and that must have been when you opened the door. I know it's hard to believe, but that's what happened. By the time I wrestled her off of me I guess you were gone.

I tried to call you the next morning and for weeks after that, but you wouldn't answer my calls and you never returned any of my messages. I even tried coming by your place and your job, but you were never there. And when we had dinner, when you said you thought we should see other people, it just didn't make sense to me. For the last couple of months I've been trying to figure out what happened with us and how I could get you back. This is the best that I could do." He paused and shrugged his shoulders. "I love you, Shelby."

I know I said I wasn't going to cry and I hadn't, yet, but I felt puddles of tears fill my eyes. I don't know if it was because of what he had just said or if it was because Julian looked so beautiful to me at that moment. I wanted to apologize to him for all the time I had wasted, but he wasn't finished yet, though.

"Shelby, for me, tonight has to be all or nothing. I know, if I do nothing I lose you forever, so the choice was easy for me. I have to play my hand."

He released my hands, reached into his jacket pocket, and pulled out a small, black, velvet jewelry box. When he opened it I saw the biggest diamond I had ever seen in my life. It was like something a girl could only dream of. It was beautiful as it sparkled in the candlelight. I inhaled as tears rolled down my cheeks. It was only when he began speaking again that I actually started breathing again.

"I want you to be my wife, Shelby. I need to know I will always have you in my life. I want you to be my best friend, my lover, my wife, the mother of my children, and anything else you think you might want to be. Will you have me? Will you marry me?"

I really don't remember saying yes, but I guess I did. After standing there crying and holding each other, we sat back down and talked for the next couple of hours. We decided we would see each other the next evening and start working on our wedding plans.

"Shelby, I don't want to wait. Let's get married as soon as possible. I don't want to waste anymore time. We've wasted enough."

"I agree. Maybe you should run the show…"

"Absolutely not! We'll do this together, and don't worry about how much it's going to cost. It's going to be a big party for our family and friends."

When we finished talking, Julian walked me to the limo and kissed me good night. As the car pulled off of the property, I sat in the backseat thinking how quickly things change.

"So, is everything going to be all right with you two?"

I showed him my hand. "We're getting married." I smiled as he turned to look at my ring.

"I knew that boy wasn't no fool. Congratulations! I told Gladys I'd dance at your wedding one day. Yes, sir, congratulations." Satisfied, Mr. Vestas started the car and began to drive off.

I sat back and pulled out my cell phone, but not before excusing myself and raising the glass partition for a little privacy.

I called Tracie. "I'm coming over. Call Kyomi and tell her to meet me at your house. I have something I want to tell both of y'all."

I knew I woke Tracie up because she sounded kind of crazy, and because it was about 2 o'clock in the morning "What? I mean what? Is everything all right?"

"Girl, everything is fine. Call...you know what? Never mind. I'll call Kyomi. Don't hang up. Hold on for a minute."

I called Kyomi and quickly clicked back over to Tracie while the phone was ringing. Of course, Kyomi was asleep too, but that didn't stop her from asking questions after she answered the phone.

"Why are you up at this time of night calling people?

I smiled at the idea of how quickly things can change. "Guess who's getting married?"

# Chapter 20

The next few weeks were a whirlwind. Julian suggested having the wedding and the reception at his house. He didn't want our parents and other family members to have to do any driving after the festivities. We met with the florist and the wedding coordinator several times to discuss the kind of flowers we wanted and where we wanted them placed throughout the house and the yard. Julian also wanted to make sure the actual ceremony was quick and that most of the time was spent enjoying the reception. He wanted everything on point and timely. We decided on a six layer, yellow and chocolate, white icing cake, with lilies and various colored tulips and greenery cascading down two sides of the cake. The groomsmen's tuxedos would be black and their cummerbunds would be multi-colored—black, white, periwinkle blue, silver, and fuchsia. The bridesmaids' dresses were periwinkle blue.

For the reception there would be sixty tent-covered tables, with table settings for eight. We decided on putting strings of little white lights on the ceiling of the tent to make the backyard cozy and romantic. The place settings that we selected were white with a platinum and gray-banded pattern. The wineglasses and the water goblets were crystal and the flatware was sterling silver. The centerpieces on the tables would be white and light blue flowers and white candles. We would also have candles placed throughout the yard and the house because the wedding would begin at sunset. The food for the reception would be catered because Miss Gladys, along with Mr. Vestas and Miss Bracie, the housekeeper, would be a guest.

Julian and I worked hard on the menu with the caterer. There would be three open bars, one in the house and two outside, and the food would be served by several waiters. Oh, yeah, we also had a gazebo built. We decided to take our vows under the gazebo, surrounded by four hundred chairs. Anybody that was late could stand up as we exchanged our vows. And, to top things off, we also put flower petals and floating candles in the pool, to add a special touch.

Julian was a doll. He helped with everything except my dress, the bridesmaids' dresses, and the dresses for our mothers and grandmothers. It goes without saying, that job was left up to me and my girls, Tracie and Kyomi. I gave them free reign with the bridesmaids' dresses because they would be wearing them. We giggled like teenagers as they playfully tried on the ugliest dresses they could find before we found just the right dress for them and my two sisters.

Trying to find a wedding dress was just as much fun, but a little more somber. I wanted to be beautiful, but I wanted something simple, yet elegant. The wedding gown I eventually chose was a white, strapless, silk-satin Mermaid dress, with a long hand-tatted, German lace hip sash decorated with white pearl and silver crystal beading, and my shoes were a pair of Christian Louboutin glitter, peep-toe, sling back pumps, which Julian had earlier surprised me with as a wedding gift.

The day I found my dress I stood in the mirror and cried. Kyomi walked up behind me and put her arms around my shoulders.

"You okay?"

I shrugged my shoulders and nodded my head. "Yeah, I just can't believe this; everything is happening so fast. I was just standing here looking at myself in the mirror and it hit me, I'm getting married…in just a few days?"

"Yeah, you are, but you know what? Everything is going to be all right." She paused and looked at my reflection in the mirror. "You're going to be a beautiful bride, you're going to have a beautiful wedding, and you're going to live happily ever after. You've found the man of your dreams and you both love each other— that's no small feat. It actually took y'all a good little while to get to this point, and I know you're both going to work very hard at keeping each other happy and making this marriage work."

Tracie walked over and put her arms around both of us. "This is the dress, so you better go in the dressing room and take it off before we cry all over it and mess it up."

I left the dress shop with my wedding gown in hand.

On the day of the wedding I was surprisingly nervous. My mom, my sisters, and my best friends were there, but I was a mess. It was still hard to believe Julian and I had made it this far. Just a month ago I was sure it was over. If it hadn't been for that phone call from Smokie I would still be thinking Julian cheated on me. It's amazing how easy it is to misinterpret a situation. I guess the saying, "Believe none of what you hear and half of what you see," does apply sometimes. In just a few short hours I would be Mrs. Julian "Jules" Brishard. Wow, it was unbelievable

"Honey!" It was my mom calling. "What are you thinking about? Didn't you hear us come into the room?"

I looked up at her and Julian's mom and smiled.

Miss Brishard looked at me and started laughing. "Are you having second thoughts?"

"She can't be any more nervous than I am. I've never been to a wedding with so many celebrities. I feel like I'm getting married." My mother laughed as she walked over to my dress hanging on the closet door.

We all laughed as Tracie, Kyomi, Kari, and Sharrin came into the room to help me get dressed. They were so pretty that it brought tears to my eyes. The entire wedding party—my mother, Julian's mom, and our grandmothers—had gotten their hair and nails done this morning. This was my way of showing them my appreciation for sharing this special day with me and Julian. We also bought a pair of ½ carat diamond studs, as well as diamond and sapphire necklaces for everyone in the wedding party. We bought the guys really nice silver and diamond cufflinks.

After my makeup was done, I put on my diamond drop earrings before the ladies began to help me put on my dress. I stood in front of the mirror and looked at myself. The first time I was married I didn't have a wedding, so this was especially exciting for me. As everyone fussed over me, I thought about what Julian said to me the first time we went to a party together, "You're going to be the center of attention, but don't worry, I'm going to be right here with you." I smiled to myself because that was nothing compared to today.

I winced. It was almost time for me to go downstairs. "Kari, do I look okay? Is everything in place?"

She stepped back and looked at me. "You're beautiful."

When I walked out the door, my niece, who was the flower girl, was sitting on the floor in the hallway outside the room. I laughed at how cute she looked. Her dress was very similar to mine. On the floor next to her was her basket filled with blue and white flower petals.

She looked up at me. "Auntie Shell, you look pretty."

"Thank you, baby." I extended my hand to help her up from the floor.

As we headed for the staircase, hand in hand, I thought, *Okay, here we go.* By the time we got to the door I could see that our mothers had been seated and I could see Julian standing up front looking 'faune.' He was stretching his neck to look down the aisle to see if he could see me. I smiled because he looked anxious, too.

My dad walked up next to me and grabbed my arm and placed it under his.

He looked down at me with tears in his eyes. "You look too beautiful to give away, baby girl." Then he kissed me on my forehead.

I guess this was it. The bride's song to the groom began to play, *I Love You,* by Angel Grant. I had to take a couple of deep breaths because my eyes began to tear up. Each bridesmaid was met at the door by her groomsman and escorted down the aisle, then the maid of honor, Sharrin, and then my matron of honor, Kari. Smokie and Kari's husband were already standing with Julian. The ring bearer, one of my nephews, went out, but not without some coaxing. It appeared that, at the last minute, he changed his mind and decided he wanted to sit down and watch the wedding.

My niece looked up at my dad. "Auntie Shell and Pappa, I'm not going to cry because I'm a big girl."

My dad looked down at her. "I know, you're Pappa's big girl."

She smiled and headed down the aisle, gently tossing flower petals from her basket as she walked. "The bride is coming. The bride is coming."

When she reached the front *The Wedding March* began to play and everyone stood up. I looked up at my dad, he smiled and patted my hand that was holding on to his forearm, and we began to slowly walk down the aisle. It seemed like I was moving in slow motion. I looked ahead at Julian. He wasn't smiling. He had a sort of funny look on his face (he later told me it was because he couldn't believe how beautiful I looked).

When we reached the front Julian gently took my hand to lead me up the stairs of the gazebo. My father kissed me on my cheek then stepped back and took his seat. The minister, David, a friend of mine, asked everyone to bow their heads so he could pray.

After praying, he quickly asked, "Who gives this woman away?"

My father proudly stood up from his seat and nervously responded. "Her mother and I do." He then sat back down.

Julian looked at him as if to say, "Yeah…"

David read some scriptures from the Bible, sharing with us the role of a husband and a wife. He talked about being fair and loving, having realistic expectations of each other. One thing that he said that I really appreciated was that we hadn't done all of this hard work and planning for just one day, but that, hopefully, we had done all of this to prepare for a long life together. He also read 1 Corinthians 13:4-7, and the first part of verse 8, about love, then he began with the wedding vows. After I said my vows I began to put Julian's ring on his finger. I thought I was going to drop it because my hands were shaking so badly. When Julian said his vows they were strong and certain. How could I have ever doubted this man's love for me? I was shaking even more when he started to put my ring on my finger. I was so nervous that I actually thought I was going to faint. Julian's smile silently reassured me everything was okay. After he slid the ring on my finger, teary-eyed, I looked up at him. We had finally done it; we were married.

Turning to look at the minister, it was his cue to say, "I now pronounce you husband and wife." I had no idea what was taking so long because this should have been the end of the wedding according to the program. Baffled, I turned my attention back to Julian and raised my eyebrows. Smokie reached into his pocket and handed Julian a cordless microphone. Julian smiled at me and began to sing:

*You are the breath that I breathe*
*Your love makes me pray*
*for more than 24 hours in a day*
*Every time I close my eyes*
*I dream dreams of fantasies*
*You, me*
*us, we*
*life, love,*
*so long, forever*
*together, together, together*
*I promise you love*
*that none can compare*
*and happiness brand new*

## Every Time I Close My Eyes

*Thank you for teaching me,*
*showing me*
*love's seed*
*planted*
*watered*
*grown*
*bloomed*
*to a forever us,*
*a forever we*
*Every time I close my eyes*
*I dream dreams of fantasies*
*You, me*
*us, we*
*life, love,*
*so long, forever*
*together, together, together*
*You are my sweet lady,*
*my sweet baby,*
*my honey,*
*my boo*
*Each day will begin and end with you*
*me*
*we*
*us*
*together, forever, forever, forever*
*ain't no end to what our love will do*
*Every time I close my eyes*
*I dream dreams of fantasies*
*you, me*
*us, we*

*life, love,*
*so long, forever*
*together, together, together*

Julian had written a song—*Every Time I Close My Eyes*—for our wedding. He was unbelievable. Was this a small indication of how the rest of our life together was going to be? If it was, I didn't think it was possible to love him any more than I did at this moment.

After the music ended, David turned his attention back to us. "I now pronounce you husband and wife. You may kiss your bride."

Everyone clapped. Julian gently placed his hands on either side of my face, as I gripped his forearms.

"I love you, Shelby."

We kissed. Finally, husband and wife.

# Chapter 21

There was really nowhere to exit to, so we walked into the house, and then went back outside for pictures. While we were having our photos taken, our guests mingled during the cocktail hour as the yard crew rearranged the chairs and brought out round tables. The wedding party's table was placed under the gazebo, so we could see and be seen by everyone at the reception. When the photographer finished, we made our way back into the house, so that the wedding party could be formally introduced during the reception.

We quietly stood at the door and listened as the wedding coordinator introduced us for the first time. "Please, everyone stand and join me in welcoming Mr. and Mrs. Julian Brishard."

Our guests applauded as we exited the house, hand in hand, and made our way down the walkway, across the dance floor, between the tables, to the stairs of the gazebo. Once there, we turned and struck a quick pose, as we had been very strongly instructed to do by the wedding coordinator. We gave each other a quick kiss, and then, as the cameras flashed, Julian escorted me up the stairs to our seats at the table with our wedding party.

As soon as we were seated, the waiters began serving the wedding party and quickly, thereafter, began serving our guests. All of the RSVP cards had been randomly assigned numbers to coordinate with the numbers on the tables, so that it would be easier for the waiters to serve the three course meal. I didn't eat very much because I really didn't have an appetite and, from the looks of things, neither did Julian.

As we both picked over our food, I leaned over and whispered in Julian's ear, "Where are going when we leave here?"

He looked at me and smiled. "It's a surprise."

"Come on, tell me."

"Mrs. Brishard, I'm not going to tell you, so you might as well stop asking." He gave me a peck on the lips and continued eating.

As we were talking and picking over our dessert, the wedding coordinator came up on the gazebo and asked if we were ready to dance. She then walked over to the band. As the band began to play she made her announcement.

"Excuse me for just a moment. I hope you all enjoyed or are enjoying your meal. We are going to continue with the activities as noted on your program. Please join me in welcoming Mr. and Mrs. Brishard to the floor for their first dance."

Everyone clapped as we made our way to the dance floor. LTD's *Love Ballad* began to play as Julian extended his hand.

"May I have this dance, Mrs. Brishard?"

I laughed. "Of course, Mr. Brishard."

As the music played Julian sang to me: "*I have never been so much / In love / Before / What a difference / A true love made in my life / So nice / So right / Lovin' you gave me somethin new / That I've never felt / Never dreamed of / Something's changed / Though it's not the / Feeling I had before / Oh, oh, oh it's much, much more…*"

Julian held me close and tight, like he would never let me go again. Though, being in his arms did little to quiet the butterflies in my stomach from the explosive anticipation of what was to come later. As the music changed, we stopped dancing and Julian escorted me over to my dad's table.

The wedding coordinator made her next announcement. "We'll now have the father-daughter dance."

Before handing me over, Julian shook my dad's hand, and then they hugged. Together, my dad and I walked back onto the dance floor.

As we danced, my dad whispered in my ear. "I told Julian he better take care of you." He smiled, and I smiled back. "All jokes aside, I want y'all to take care of each other, okay?" He then kissed me on the cheek.

As a lone tear rolled down my cheek, I nodded okay.

My dad led me by my hand back over to the stairs of the gazebo as the wedding coordinator announced the mother-son dance and Julian escorted his mother to the dance floor.

Once all of the programmed dances were completed, the floor was opened up to the guests, and for the next couple of hours everyone partied hard. By the end of the night I was exhausted. I would have been satisfied with staying at Julian's house and kicking everybody else out, but it was Julian's idea to make our wedding day as convenient as possible for our family and friends. The house was the perfect place for a wedding, a wedding reception, and a make-shift hotel.

Julian still hadn't told me where we were going for our honeymoon, but the plan was, some time during the reception, Julian and I were going to sneak out and drive to the airport to catch a flight to who knows where and, in the meantime, our families would stay at the house and relax. Julian had thoroughly thought out every step of his master plan. In addition to the Loubotin's he had bought for me  as a wedding gift, he also gave me $8,000 to go shopping for a new wardrobe to wear during the honeymoon. He had given me very explicit instructions about how the money was to be spent. I was to buy clothes, shoes, lingerie and anything else that I needed for a honeymoon in warm weather. I wasn't supposed to spend the money on anything for the wedding or on a gift for him.

Kyomi, Tracie, and I had a great time shopping for two weeks worth of warm weather clothes and accessories. The only thing I didn't have to spend money on was lingerie because I had received enough lingerie at my bridal shower to last an entire month. It was going to be fun trying to wear it all.

As Julian walked around mingling and talking, I watched Smokie and Sharrin. They seemed to make a really cute couple together. Ironically, they appeared to have a calming effect on each another. I smiled when I thought about Smokie and how far he and I had come. It goes without saying, I didn't dislike him anymore. As a matter of fact, I was rather fond of him now. I could only reflect on the words Miss Gladys told me a long time ago: "Smokie is a nice boy." I guess she was right. If it hadn't been for Smokie, Julian and I probably would not have spoken to each other again, and that would have been a really sad way to end things. Instead, here we are at our wedding reception.

Speaking of which, as I looked around the yard it was beautiful. The backyard was strewn with white table clothed tables adorned with centerpieces of white candles, white tulips, periwinkle blue iris, and greenery, and the bridesmaids were absolutely beautiful in their silk-satin, periwinkle blue, spaghetti strapped dresses. It all looked like a scene from a fantasy. My sisters were absolutely gorgeous and my brothers were also very handsome in their tuxedos. Poor Coco was going to kill himself trying to dance with all the single women at the reception. That boy worried me…looking for a woman, but looking at all the wrong things.

Julian's mother and grandmother were sitting at a table with my parents talking. It was nice to see them enjoying each other's company. It was my understanding, Julian's mom and grandmother had made plans to spend their next vacation at my parents' home. And the other guests, they all seemed to be enjoying themselves, as well. As I continued to look around, I saw Julian across the yard. He winked at me and smiled. He looked just as good today, our wedding day, as he did the first day we met. I teared up as I gazed at him. I love that man...my husband.

# Chapter 22

For the entire reception I kept waiting for Julian to sneak up behind me and grab my hand, so that we could make a quick getaway to the airport, but it never happened. The wedding ceremony began at sunset and was finished in 30 minutes. The reception started immediately after the cocktail hour. At 10:00 p.m. we cut the cake. I thought, for sure, we would sneak out after that, but it didn't happen. At 11:30 p.m. Julian and I danced.

Julian held me close and whispered in my ear. "Are you tired?"

I smiled. "Are you?"

He stood back and looked at me and shook his head. "Uh, huh."

So I thought, *Oh, good, this must be the cue to leave*, but, instead, we kept right on dancing. Then Smokie stepped in and he and I danced for a while.

"You are a beautiful bride, Shelby."

"Thanks…" I pretended to clear my throat. "…Omar."

He laughed. "Look, I've never seen my boy this happy and I know it's because of you." He paused. "I don't know what it is, but seeing him like this makes me think this is something I want one day, too."

"What, a big wedding?"

"No, I mean what y'all have. When y'all look at each other it's crazy—you give off a vibe. That's what I'm talking about. People can live off the love y'all have leftover. It's a trip."

"You can have the same thing. You just have to be open and honest—show what you have inside. You know that, though, right?" I smiled and gave him a hug. "You'll find it."

After Smokie and I finished dancing, I found Julian and we sat down at our table. Several guests walked up to talk with us and to congratulate us. While we were sitting there, our parents walked over to give us more hugs and to say goodnight. By the time midnight rolled around I was too tired to even care about leaving and, frankly, I was a little irked that we were still at the house. I knew our luggage had been in the car all day, but all I could think about now was getting out of my dress and going to sleep.

Julian looked at me and kissed me on my cheek and reached for my hand. "Give me your hand."

"Uh, uh…I don't want to dance again."

He laughed. "Just let me hold your hand, girl."

He pulled me to my feet and led me through the crowd into the house. I stopped when we reached the staircase.

"Where are we going, Julian?"

He didn't utter a word as he led me upstairs to the master bedroom. When he opened the door the room had been filled with candles, the bed had been turned back, and one of my new nighties was on the bed.

I turned and looked at Julian. "What's going on?"

Julian closed the door and locked it behind him. "You looked tired. I thought you might want to go to bed."

I was confused because I had been expecting to leave all night and instead we were still at the house, in the bedroom.

"So, we're not going anywhere?"

Julian walked over, stood in front of me, and looked down at me. "I'll wake you up when it's time to go."

I was too tired to ask any more questions, so I took a shower, put on my nightie, and went to bed. Julian held me in his arms as we both fell asleep. I guess he was tired, too.

# Chapter 23

The next morning, I woke up to the sound of Julian's voice. "Wake up, Shell. It's time to go."

Whining, I rolled over on my stomach. "What time is it?"

Julian laughed as he pulled me out of the bed. "Come on, girl, you don't want to miss the plane do you?"

I got up, even though all I wanted to do was sleep. When I looked at the clock I realized why I was so sleepy. It was only 4 o'clock in the morning. I got up and drug myself into the bathroom, brushed my teeth, and found some clothes to put on. Someone had graciously taken a sundress out of my suitcase for me. I'm pretty sure everybody, except me, knew what was going on.

We got into the limo at exactly 4:45. I laid my head on Julian's shoulder and fell back asleep. I was too sleepy to ask where we were flying off to. When we got to the airport Julian woke me up and we walked straight to the gate. I realized later he had sent our luggage ahead. When we reached the gate I noticed the sign read Miami, so I made the most logical conclusion. I still didn't ask any questions because if we were going to spend our honeymoon in Coconut Grove that was cool with me. It was a 6:37 a.m. flight and, frankly, I still wasn't in the mood to hold a conversation.

By the time we landed in Miami I was a little more alert. Julian and I held hands as we walked through the terminal to board our connecting flight. Because it was still relatively early, only a few people stopped us and asked for his autograph. He was relieved that his new wife didn't have to deal with his normal fanfare. It could be intimidating and overwhelming to have people constantly approaching for autographs, and the like, so he planned the flights early in the morning for my benefit. My man, always thinking on his feet.

I eventually figured out our destination—the West Indies. On our connecting flight we talked about how smoothly the wedding and the reception had gone. We were both anxious to see the wedding pictures when we returned to the States. Julian felt the same way I did—it was hard to believe everything we had gone through in the last few months.

Julian looked up from the magazine he was thumbing through. "You know, Shell, I knew I had to marry you because I couldn't stop thinking about you when I couldn't find you, but even before then I knew. When you wouldn't call me back, I thought for sure you had found somebody else." He paused, "I missed you so much. It was crazy."

I put my finger up to his lips. "I missed you, too. I promise, that won't ever happen again...ever."

We kissed, and then talked until the plane landed at the Hewanorra Airport in St. Lucia. We rented a Range Rover at the airport and drove to Petit Piton. Julian still wouldn't tell me exactly where we were going, so I excitedly admired the plush jungle terrain as we rode to our destination.

"Shell, remember, when we first started hanging out with each other, when we were still meeting at the restaurant for dinner?"

I smiled at him and rubbed the back of his head.

"One night I asked you where you'd go if you just wanted to get away from everything to relax. You told me..."

"I told you I would go to an island and hide away in an open-air cottage that overlooked...an ocean..." I stopped and looked at him. "You remember that?"

He laughed. "Girl, I remember everything you've ever said to me."

As he spoke, I looked around at the sprawling estates that we were passing. Any one of them could be where we were going to spend our honeymoon. Instead, we rode until we came to a beautiful green cottage with orange shutters, surrounded by ginger and bird of paradise. Julian practically rode up to the front door before he stopped. I quickly got out of the truck and walked toward the house. I immediately realized it overlooked the Caribbean Sea. Julian had done this because of a conversation we had when we first met. I shook my head in disbelief and, of course, I started crying.

Julian walked over and put his arms around me. "Are you all right, baby?"

I turned around and kissed him. "This is amazing. This is amazing. I can't believe you were able to do this. Thank you."

Julian smiled. "Anything for you."

I hugged him from the back as we entered the cute, little cottage. "You sure you don't want to carry me over the threshold?"

"Uh, uh, nope." He laughed and wrapped his arms around his back and grabbed me.

The inside of the house looked exactly like I had imagined—an open living room, a large kitchen, and beautiful live flower arrangements throughout the house. Adjacent to the kitchen was a veranda with a dining table on one side and a large hammock on the other side. Down the stairs from the veranda was a large pool. The master bedroom had a king size, four poster bed and French doors that opened up to a terrace. There was also a huge ensuite bathroom.

Julian followed me through the house and watched as I took everything in. "We're near a volcano, several botanical gardens, a few mineral baths, and a beach. So, we're not going to run out of things to do."

I heard him, but I was still in awe that he had gone through such great lengths to make our honeymoon so special.

While we were standing in the doorway between the veranda and the kitchen, I turned and looked him. "How did you find this place?"

He took a deep breath. "Well, It really wasn't that difficult. I know some folks that spend a lot of time in the Caribbean, so I asked them if they knew of any places like this on any of the islands. They gave me the name of a realtor; I contacted her; flew down here to check out a few places; and the rest is history."

"I have to keep my eye on you. You're sneaky, Mr. Brishard."

We didn't have to spend any time unpacking because someone had already done that for us. Julian had also arranged to have an on-call cook for most of our stay, even though we weren't that far from the local restaurants. It wasn't long before he sprang his next surprise on me.

"Okay, wife, freshen up because we're going out for lunch."

"Really, you don't want to just sit down and kick your feet up...or something?"

I was sort of baffled that Julian wanted to leave the house so soon after arriving. We've been together almost two years and we've never made love and now that we're married I thought, for sure, that's what would be on his mind. Maybe I was more anxious about it than he was.

As we drove to the restaurant I admired the plush, green trees of the island. It didn't take long to arrive to our destination. Lunch at the Caribbean Gardens restaurant was fantastic. All during lunch I couldn't stop looking at Julian.

After lunch we took a walk around town and did a little sightseeing. By the time we got back to the cottage it was 5:00 p.m. We hopped out of the Range Rover and playfully strolled around the property. I was happier than I had been in years. I had come to realize I was in control of my own happiness. I couldn't depend on Julian or anyone else for that. I'm pretty sure that was the lesson I learned. Now, I was able to, again, share myself with someone else and trust that he would share himself with me. It was a big relief to have freed myself to give and receive love again. As I was musing, Julian walked up behind me and put his arms around my waist.

"What are you thinking about?"

I looked at him over my right shoulder. "Nothing…I'm just happy to be here…with you."

He kissed me on the cheek and grabbed my hand. "Come on, let's go inside."

Before we settled in for the night we took the time to find out where our clothes had been put. After Julian found his he jumped in the shower. He came out of the bathroom in a pair of silk, maroon pajama bottoms and hopped straight in the bed.

He smiled at me and patted the bed next to him. "When are you coming to bed?"

I turned my back and laughed. "I don't know. It's still kind of early. I was thinking I'd read for a couple of hours, and then come to bed after that."

"Oh, okay. Wake me up when you finish reading."

I smiled at him then turned and quietly walked into the bathroom to take a shower. After my shower I took my time as I oiled my body from head to toe, combed my hair back, and dabbed on just a little bit of perfume. I felt like a virgin on my wedding night. The idea of that made me giggle to myself. The truth was, it had been a little over three years since the last time I had made love. I took a deep breath and looked at myself in the mirror one last time before I turned off the bathroom light and opened the door.

Julian had turned off the lights and there were candles all over the bedroom. I stood in the doorway of the bathroom and looked at him. I loved the way he looked back at me.

As he hungrily looked me up and down, he got up and sat on the edge of the bed. "Come here…"

Without breaking my gaze, I slowly walked over to him. As I stood there he placed his hands on my waist and kissed my stomach. Then he laid his head on my belly and held me. His hands moved up my calves, to the back of my thighs, and then to the small of my back. A shiver ran through my body as he stood up behind me. He ran his hands up both of my arms and stopped at my shoulders. My breathing became labored as my body responded to his touch.

Julian playfully whispered in my ear. "Why are you shaking? You nervous?"

With my eyes closed, I bit my bottom lip and shook my head. Julian kissed me on both of my shoulders then on either side of my neck. One at a time, I felt my straps fall from my shoulders, and in one swift movement my nightie fell to the floor. Julian's hands were all over my body. It felt so good that I thought I was going to pass out. It was finally going to happen. Julian picked me up and placed me on the bed. As we kissed, each of his movements was slow and concise. He gave attention to every nook, cranny, and crevice of my body. After that, it seemed like we made love for hours. It felt like every nerve in my body had been awakened.

When it was over, we quietly lie there out of breath and covered in sweat. As I rested in Julian's arms he brushed my hair from my face.

"You okay?"

I nodded my head. "Uh, huh...yeah. You?"

With his finger under my chin he leaned over and kissed me on the lips. We both fell asleep, waking up several times during the night to make love again, and again, and again...

The next morning we were awakened up by the smell of breakfast. It was kind of strange knowing someone had been in the house cooking while we were asleep, but if Julian was comfortable with the arrangement so was I. We put our robes on, brushed our teeth, washed our faces, and went into the kitchen. I didn't know about Julian, but I would have preferred to stay in the bed for a little while longer.

We found toasted English muffins, scrambled eggs, and bacon on the stove and fresh fruit and juice on the counter. The cook had placed two place settings, as well as fresh flowers, on the table on the veranda, so we fixed our plates and went outside to enjoy our meal.

As we were eating I looked across the table at Julian. "So what do you have planned for us today?"

Julian looked up from his plate. "I don't know about you, but all I want to do today is make love, eat, sleep, and make love some more." He smiled mischievously as he bit on a piece of bacon.

"Oh, I think that's doable."

Julian excused himself from the table to call the company that sent the cook over. He arranged to have the cook come back to prepare dinner around 6:00 p.m., as well breakfast and dinner the next day. We spent the next couple of days hold up in the cottage. When we eventually ventured away from the house, we walked the beach, visited some of the botanical gardens, and soaked in the mineral springs. We took hundreds of pictures to share with our family and friends.

I couldn't believe our last morning on the island rolled around so quickly.

"Julian, let's stay another week."

Laughing, he pulled me up against his chest. "You know we can do everything we did here at home." When he released me he patted my butted and walked out of the room.

As we boarded the plane, I knew our honeymoon was officially over. When we arrived at the airport in Miami someone recognized Julian. Fortunately, he had scheduled fans into our travel plans this time, so we had more than enough time for him to sign autographs and for us to get from one flight to the next. I guess this was the beginning of our life together and my life as a celebrity's wife. It was obvious that someone had also leaked our return to the press. Paparazzi and fans were everywhere when we landed at our final destination. Women were holding up signs that read: "We love you Jules, Congratulations!" and "We Missed You, Welcome Home!"

Smokie was waiting for us, along with Julian's bodyguards. They got us through the crowd and escorted us to the limo. Even though I had experienced the frenzied atmosphere at his concerts, I still couldn't believe how the women were swarming around us.

"Julian, is it always like that?" As we made our way to the car, I held onto his arm tight.

"I always take the earliest or the latest flights for just that very reason, to try to avoid crowds as much as possible."

As I looked out the car window at the crowd, I thought: *Really, what had I gotten myself into? I hoped this was as bad as it was ever going to get.* Julian must have known what I was thinking because he grabbed my hand and kissed me on the cheek.

"You don't have to worry about a thing. I'm going to make sure our life is very private and that you and the kids are always safe."

*Kids? What 'kids?*

I looked up at him. He smiled and winked his eye at me as the car pulled away from the curb.

## About the Author

T.R. Baker is a judicial assistant for a DeKalb County, Georgia, State Court Judge. Her debut novel, *Every Time I Close My Eyes*, was originally released in January 2003. Since that time she has written and is preparing to release four more novels: *Daddy's Big Girl, Yet to be Determined, Sold Sister,* and *Double Vision,* the sequel to *Every Time I Close My Eyes.* She also still has aspirations to release a book of poetry titled *Amongst Friends.*

Catch the author at:

www.simplytrbaker.com
www.simplytrb.blogspot.com
www.facebook.com/tayarbaker2
https://twitter.com/suprtay